PHILIP K. DICK

# THE COSMIC PUPPETS

Philip K. Dick was born in Chicago in 1928 and lived most of his life in California. He briefly attended the University of California, but dropped out before completing any classes. In 1952, he began writing professionally and proceeded to write numerous novels and short-story collections. He won the Hugo Award for the best novel in 1962 for *The Man in the High Castle* and the John W. Campbell Memorial Award for best novel of the year in 1974 for *Flow My Tears, the Policeman Said*. Philip K. Dick died on March 2, 1982, in Santa Ana, California, of heart failure following a stroke.

## NOVELS BY PHILIP K. DICK

# THE COSMIC PUPPETS

# THE

# COSMIC

# PUPPETS

PHILIP K. DICK

VINTAGE BOOKS
A Division of Random House, Inc.
New York

FIRST VINTAGE BOOKS EDITION, NOVEMBER 2003

The Cataloging-in-Publication Data is on file
at the Library of Congress.

**Vintage ISBN 1-4000-3005-6**

www.vintagebooks.com

Printed in the United States of America
10 9 8 7 6 5 4 3 2 1

# THE COSMIC PUPPETS

# ONE

Peter Trilling watched quietly as the other children played in the dust by the side of the porch. They were intent on their game. Mary was carefully kneading and shaping brown lumps of clay into vague shapes. Noaks sweated furiously to keep up with her. Dave and Walter had already finished theirs and were resting. Abruptly, Mary tossed her black hair, arched her slim body, and set down a clay goat.

'See?' She demanded. 'Where's yours?'

Noaks hung his head; his hands were too slow and clumsy to keep up with the girl's flying fingers. Mary had already swept up her clay goat and was rapidly reshaping it into a horse.

'Look at mine,' Noaks muttered thickly. He stood a clumsily formed airplane on its tail and gave it an accompanying noise with wet lips.'See? Pretty good, huh?'

Dave snorted. 'That's lousy. Look at this.' He pushed his clay sheep forward, close to Walter's dog.

Peter watched silently. Aloof from the other children, he sat curled up on the bottom step of the porch, arms folded, dark brown eyes liquid and huge. His tousled, sandy-colored hair hung down around his wide forehead. His cheeks were deeply tanned from the hot midsummer sun. He was a small child, thin and long-limbed; his neck was bony and his ears strangely shaped. He said very little; he liked to sit and watch the others.

'What's that?' Noaks demanded.

'A cow.' Mary shaped the legs of her cow and set it on

the ground beside Noaks' airplane. Noaks saw it with awe; he drew back unhappily, one hand on his airplane. Then he lifted it up and soared it plaintively.

Doctor Meade and Mrs Trilling came down the stairs of the boarding house together. Peter drew aside, out of the doctor's way; he carefully avoided contact with the blue pin-striped trouser leg, black shiny shoes. 'Okay,' Doctor Meade said briskly to his daughter, as he glanced at his gold pocket watch. 'Time to go back up to Shady House.'

Mary got reluctantly to her feet. 'Can't I stay?'

Doctor Meade put his arm around his daughter affectionately. 'Get going, you little Wanderer. Into the car.' He turned back to Mrs Trilling, again professional. 'There's nothing to worry about. Probably pollen from the broom plants. They're flowering now.'

'Those yellow things?' Mrs Trilling dabbed at her streaming eyes. Her plump face was swollen and red, eyes half-closed. 'They didn't do it last year.'

'Allergies are strange,' Doctor Meade said vaguely. He chewed on the stump of his cigar. 'Mary, I told you to get in the car.' He opened the door and slid in behind the wheel. 'Give me a call, Mrs Trilling, if those antihistamine pills don't do the trick. I'll probably be over tonight for dinner, anyhow.'

Nodding and wiping her eyes, Mrs Trilling disappeared back inside the boarding house, to the hot kitchen and the piles of dishes left over from lunch. Mary moved sullenly toward the station wagon, hands deep in the pockets of her jeans. 'That ruins the game,' she muttered.

Peter slid off his step. 'I'll play,' he said quietly. He picked up Mary's discarded clay and began to reshape it.

Boiling summer sun streamed down on the hilly farms, the acres of wild brush and trees, the jutting cedars and laurels and poplars. And pines, of course. They were leaving Patrick County, getting close to Carroll and the jutting projection of Beamer Knob. The road was in bad repair. The sleek yellow Packard coughed and hesitated as it pushed up the steep Virginia hills.

'Ted, let's go back,' Peggy Barton groaned. 'I've had all I can take.' She hunched over and rummaged for a can of beer behind the seat. The can was warm. She dropped it back in the sack and settled sullenly against the door, beads of perspiration on her cheeks, arms folded furiously.

'Later,' Ted Barton murmured. He had rolled down the window and hung as far out as he could, a rapt, excited look on his face. His wife's voice made no impression on him: his complete attention was on the road ahead, and what lay beyond the next hills. 'Not much farther,' he added, presently.

'You and your damn town!'

'I wonder how it'll look. You know, Peg, it's been eighteen years. I was only nine when my family moved away to Richmond. I wonder if anybody'll remember me. That old teacher, Miss Baines. And the Negro gardener who took care of our place. Doctor Dolan. All kinds of people.'

'Probably dead.' Peg pulled herself up and tugged peevishly at the open collar of her blouse. Her dark hair hung moistly against her neck; drops of perspiration slid down her breasts, over her pale skin. She had taken off her shoes and stockings and rolled up her sleeves. Her skirt was wrinkled and grimy with dust. Flies buzzed around the car; one landed on her gleaming arm and she slapped at it wildly. 'What a hell of a way to spend a vacation! We might as well have stayed in New York and suffered. At least there was something to drink.'

Ahead, the hills rose sharply. The Packard stalled, then pushed on as Barton shifted into low. Immense peaks lifted against the horizon; they were getting near the Appalachians. Barton's eyes were wide with awe as the forests and mountains came nearer, old sights, familiar peaks and valleys and twists he hadn't ever expected to see again.

'Millgate is on the floor of a small valley,' he murmured. 'Mountains on all sides. Only this one road goes in, unless they've built more since I left. It's a small town, honey. Sleepy and ordinary like a hundred other little towns. Two hardware stores, drugstores, blacksmith shop – '

'Any bars? *Please* say it has a good bar!'

'Not more than a few thousand people. Not many cars come this way. These farms aren't much good, around here. The soil's too rocky. Snows in the winter and gets hot as hell in the summer.'

'No kidding,' Peg muttered. Her flushed cheeks had gone white; she looked greenish around the lips. 'Ted, I think I'm going to be carsick.'

'We'll be there soon,' Barton answered vaguely. He hung farther out the window, craning his neck and trying to make out the scenery ahead. 'By golly, there's that old farmhouse! I remember that. And this cut-off.' He turned from the main road onto a smaller side road. 'It's just over this ridge and then we're there.'

The Packard picked up speed. It raced between dry fields and sagging fences. The road was cracked and weed-covered, broken and in bad repair. Narrow and sharp-turning.

Barton pulled his head inside. 'I knew I'd find my way back here.' He fumbled in his coat pocket and got out his lucky compass. 'It led me back, Peg. My dad gave me this when I was eight. Got it at Berg's Jewelry Store on Central

Street. The only jewelry store in Millgate. I can always depend on it. I've carried this little compass around with me, and – '

'I know,' Peg groaned wearily. 'I've heard about it a million times.'

Barton lovingly put the little silver compass away. He gripped the wheel tight and peered ahead, his excitement growing as the car neared Millgate. 'I know every inch of this road. You know, Peg, I remember once – '

'Yes, you remember. My God, I wish you'd forget at least *something*. I'm so tired of hearing all the details of your childhood, all the lovely facts about Millgate, Virginia – sometimes I just feel like screaming!'

The road plunged around a steep curve, into a thick bank of haze. With his foot on the brake, Barton turned the nose of the Packard down and began to descend.

'There she is,' he said softly. 'Look.'

Below them was a small valley, lost in the blue haze of midday. A stream wound among the dark green, a ribbon of black. Webs of dirt roads. Houses, a cluster in the center. Millgate itself. The massive, somber bowl of mountains that surrounded the valley on all sides. Barton's heart thudded with painful excitement. *His town* – where he'd been born, raised, spent his childhood. He had never expected to see it again. While he and Peg were vacationing, driving through Baltimore, the idea had suddenly come. A quick cut-off at Richmond. To see it again, see how it had changed . . .

Millgate loomed ahead. Clumps of dusty brown houses and stores lined the road. Signs. A filling station. Cafes. A couple of road-houses, cars parked in the lots. *Golden Glow Beer*. The Packard swept past a drugstore, a dingy post office, and abruptly came out in the center of the town.

Side streets. Old houses. Parked cars. Bars and cheap

9

hotels. People moving slowly along. Farmers. White shirts of store owners. A tea room. Furniture store. Two grocery stores. A big market, fruit and vegetables.

Barton slowed down at a traffic light. He turned onto a side street and passed a small grammar school. A few kids were playing basketball on a dusty field. More houses, larger and well built. A fat middle-aged woman in a shapeless dress watering her garden. A team of horses.

'Well?' Peg demanded. 'Say something! How does it look to you?'

Barton didn't answer. He gripped the wheel with one hand; he was leaning out of the window, face blank. At the next cut-off he turned the car to the right and came out again on the highway. A moment later the Packard was moving slowly back among the drugstores, bars, cafes and filling stations. And still Barton hadn't answered.

Peg felt a chill of uneasiness. There was something on her husband's face that frightened her. A look she had never seen before. 'What's wrong?' she demanded. 'Has it all changed? Doesn't it look familiar?'

Barton's lips moved. 'It must be,' he muttered thickly. 'I took the right turn . . . I remember the ridge and the hills.'

Peg caught his arm. 'Ted, what's wrong?'

Barton's face was waxen. 'I've never seen this town before,' he muttered huskily, almost inaudibly. 'It's completely different.' He turned to his wife, bewildered and scared. 'This isn't the Millgate I remember. This isn't the town I grew up in!'

# TWO

Barton brought the car to a halt. With shaking hands he pushed the door open and jumped down on the blazing pavement.

Nothing was familiar. All strange. Alien. This town was not the Millgate he had known. He could feel the difference. He had never been here in his life.

The hardware store next to the bar. It was old, an ancient wood building, leaning and sagging, its yellow paint peeled off. He could make out a dim interior, harnesses, farm equipment, tools, cans of paint, faded calendars on the walls. Behind the fly-specked window was a display of fertilizers and chemical sprays. Dead insects lay in heaps in the corners. Spider webs. Warped cardboard signs. It was an old store – old as hell.

He pulled the rusty screen door open and entered. A little dried-up old man sat behind the counter like a wrinkled spider, crouched in the shadows on his stool. Steel-rimmed glasses, vest, suspenders. A litter of papers and pencil stubs around him. The interior of the store was chill and dim, and incredibly cluttered. Barton made his way through the rows of dusty merchandise, up to the old man. His heart was hammering wildly. 'Look here,' he croaked.

The old man looked up nearsightedly. 'You want something?'

'How long have you been here?'

The old man raised an eyebrow. 'What do you mean?'

'This store! This place! How long have you been here?'

The old man was silent a moment. Then he lifted a gnarled hand and pointed to a plate on the ancient brass cash-register. 1927. The store had opened for business twenty-six years ago.

Twenty-six years ago Barton had been a year old. This store had been here while he grew up. His early years, as a child, growing up in Millgate. But he had never seen this store before. And he'd never seen this old man.

'How long have you lived in Millgate?' Barton demanded.

'Forty years.'

'Do you know me?'

The old man grunted angrily. 'Never seen you before in my life.' He lapsed into sullen silence and nervously ignored Barton.

'I'm Ted Barton. Joe Barton's kid. Remember Joe Barton? Big guy, broad shoulders, black hair? Used to live on Pine Street. We had a house there. Don't you remember me?' Sudden terror knifed at him. 'The old park! Where is it? I used to play there. The old Civil War cannon. The Douglas Street school. When did they tear it down? Stazy's Meat Market; what happened to Mrs Stazy? Is she dead?'

The little old man had got slowly up from his stool. 'You must have sunstroke, young fellow. There ain't any Pine Street, not around here.'

Barton sagged. 'They changed the name?'

The old man rested his yellowed hands on the counter and faced Barton defiantly. 'I been here forty years. Longer than you been born. There never was any Pine Street around here, and no Douglas Street. There's a little park, but it don't amount to much. Maybe you been out in the sun too long. Maybe you better go lie down someplace.' He eyed Barton with suspicion and fear. 'You go see Doc Meade. You're kinda mixed up.'

Dazed, Barton left the store. Blazing sunlight spilled over him as he reached the sidewalk. He wandered along, hands in his pockets. The little old grocery store across the street. He strained to remember. What had been there? Something else. Not a grocery store. What was it . . .

A shoe store. Boots, saddles, leather goods. That was it. Doyle's Leather Goods. Hides tanned. Luggage. He had bought a belt there, a present for his father.

He crossed the street and entered the grocery store. Flies buzzed around the piles of fruit and vegetables. Dusty canned goods. A wheezing refrigerator in the back. A wire basket of eggs.

A fat middle-aged woman nodded pleasantly to him. 'Afternoon. What can I do for you?'

Her smile was sympathetic. Barton said thickly, 'I'm sorry to bother you. I used to live here, in this town. I'm looking for something. A place.'

'A place? What place?'

'A store.' His lips almost refused to frame the words. 'Doyle's Leather Goods. Does the name mean anything to you?'

Perplexity crossed the woman's broad face. 'Where was it? On Jefferson Street?'

'No,' Barton muttered. 'Right here on Central. Where I'm standing.'

Fear replaced perplexity. 'I don't understand, mister. We've been here since I was a child. My family built this store in 1889. I've been here all my life.'

Barton moved back toward the door. 'I see.'

The woman came anxiously after him. 'Maybe you're in the wrong place. Maybe you're looking for some other town. How long ago did you say . . .'

* * *

13

Her voice faded, as Barton pushed out onto the street. He came to a sign post and read it without comprehension. Jefferson Street.

This wasn't Central. He was on the wrong street. Sudden hope flickered. He'd got on the wrong street somehow. Doyle's was on Central – and this was Jefferson. He looked quickly around. Which way was Central? He began to run, slowly at first, then faster. He turned a corner and came out on a small side street. Drab bars, run-down hotels and smoke shops.

He stopped a passer-by. 'Where's Central?' he demanded. 'I'm looking for Central Street. I must have got lost.'

The man's thin face glittered with suspicion. 'Go on,' he said, and hurried off. A drunk lounging against the weatherbeaten side of a bar laughed loudly.

Barton floundered in terror. He stopped the next person, a young girl hurrying along with a package under her arm. 'Central!' he gasped. 'Where's Central Street?'

Giggling, the girl ran off. A few yards away she halted and shouted back, 'There isn't any Central Street!'

'No Central Street,' an old woman muttered, shaking her head as she passed Barton. Others agreed, not even pausing, but hurrying on.

The drunk laughed again, then belched. 'No Central,' he muttered. 'They'll all tell you that, mister. Everybody knows there's no such street.'

'There must be,' Barton answered desperately. 'There must be!'

He stood in front of the house he had been born in. Only it wasn't his house anymore. It was a huge, rambling hotel instead of a small white and red bungalow. And the street wasn't Pine Street. It was Fairmount.

14

He came to the newspaper office. It wasn't the *Millgate Weekly* anymore. Now it was the *Millgate Times*. And it wasn't a square gray concrete structure. It was a yellowed, sagging, two-story house of boards and tar paper, a converted apartment house.

Barton entered.

'Can I help you?' the young man behind the counter asked pleasantly. 'You wanted to place an ad?' He fumbled for a pad. 'Or was it a subscription?'

'I want information,' Barton answered. 'I want to see some old papers. June 1926.'

The young man blinked. He was plump and soft-looking in a white shirt, open at the neck. Pressed slacks and carefully cut fingernails. '1926? I'm afraid anything older than a year is stored down in the – '

'Get it,' Barton grated. He tossed a ten-dollar bill on the counter. 'Hurry up!'

The youth swallowed, hesitated, then scuttled through the doorway like a frightened rat.

Barton threw himself down at a table and lit a cigarette. As he was stubbing out the first butt and lighting a second, the youth reappeared, red-faced and panting, lugging a massive board-bound book. 'Here it is.' He dropped it on the table with a crash and straightened up in relief. 'Anything else you want to see, just – '

'Okay,' Barton grunted. With shaking fingers, he began turning the ancient yellowed sheets. 16 June 1926. The day of his birth. He found it, turned to the births and deaths, and traced the columns rapidly.

There it was. Black type on the yellow paper. His fingers touched it, his lips moved silently. They had his father's name as Donald, not Joe. And the address was wrong. 1386 Fairmount instead of 1724 Pine. His mother's name was given as Sarah Barton instead of Ruth. But the

15

important part was there. Theodore Barton, weight six pounds, eleven ounces, at the county hospital. But that was wrong, too. It was twisted, distorted. All garbled.

He closed the book and carried it over to the counter. 'One more. Give me the papers for October 1935.'

'Sure,' the youth answered. He hurried through the doorway. In a few moments he was back.

October 1935. The month he and his family had sold their house and pulled out. Moved to Richmond. Barton sat down at the table and turned the pages slowly. 9 October. There was his name. He scanned the column rapidly . . . And his heart stopped beating. Everything came to a complete standstill. There was no time, no motion.

### SCARLET FEVER STRIKES AGAIN

Second child dies. Water hole closed by State Health Authorities. Theodore Barton, 9, son of Donald and Sarah Barton, 1386 Fairmount Street, died at his home at seven o'clock this morning. This makes the second fatality reported, and the sixth victim in this area for a period of . . .

Mindlessly, Barton got to his feet. He didn't even remember leaving the newspaper office; the next thing he knew he was outside on the blinding hot street. People moved past. Buildings. He was walking. He turned a corner, passed unfamiliar stores. Stumbled, half-fell against a man, continued blindly on.

Finally he found himself approaching his yellow Packard. Peg emerged from the swirling haze around him. She gave a cry of wild relief.

'*Ted!*' She ran excitedly toward him, breasts heaving under her sweat-stained blouse. 'Good Lord, what's the idea of running off and leaving me? You nearly scared me out of my mind!'

16

Barton got numbly into the car and behind the wheel. Silently, he inserted the key and started up the motor.

Peg slid quickly in beside him. 'Ted, what *is* it? You're so pale. Are you sick?'

He drove aimlessly out into the street. He didn't see the people and cars. The Packard gained speed rapidly, much too rapidly. Vague shapes swarmed on all sides.

'Where are we going?' Peg demanded. 'Are we getting out of this place?'

'Yes.' He nodded. 'Out of this place.'

Peg collapsed with relief. 'Thank God. Will I be glad to get back to civilization.' She touched his arm in alarm. 'Do you want me to drive? Maybe you'd better rest. You look as if something dreadful happened. Can't you tell me?'

Barton didn't answer. He didn't even hear her. The headline seemed to hang a few feet in front of his face, the black type, yellow paper.

### SCARLET FEVER STRIKES AGAIN

Second child dies . . .

The second child was Ted Barton. He hadn't moved out of Millgate on 9 October 1935. He had died of scarlet fever. But it wasn't possible! He was alive. Sitting here in his Packard beside his grimy, perspiring wife.

Maybe he wasn't Ted Barton.

False memories. Even his name, his identity. The whole contents of his mind – everything. Falsified, by someone or something. His hands gripped the wheel desperately. But if he wasn't Ted Barton – *then who was he?*

He reached for his lucky compass. A nightmare, everything swirling around him. His compass; where was

17

it? Even that was gone. *Not gone.* Something else in his pocket.

His hand brought out a tiny bit of dry bread, hard and stale. A wad of dry bread instead of his silver compass.

# THREE

Peter Trilling squatted down and picked up Mary's discarded clay. Rapidly, he pushed the cow into a shapeless mass and began to re-form it.

Noaks and Dave and Walter regarded him with outraged incredulity. 'Who said *you* could play?' Dave demanded angrily.

'It's my yard,' Peter answered mildly. His clay shape was practically ready. He set it down in the dust beside Dave's sheep and the crude dog Walter had formed. Noaks continued to fly his airplane, ignoring Peter's creation.

'What is it?' Walter demanded angrily. 'Doesn't look like anything.'

'It's a man.'

'A man! That's a man?'

'Go on,' Dave sneered. 'You're too young to play. Go inside and your mother'll give you a cookie.'

Peter didn't answer. He was concentrating on his clay man, brown eyes large and intense. His small body was utterly rigid; he leaned forward, face down, lips moving faintly.

For a moment nothing happened. Then . . .

Dave shrieked and scrambled away. Walter cursed loudly, face suddenly white. Noaks stopped flying his airplane. His mouth fell open and he sat frozen.

The little clay man had stirred. Faintly at first, then more energetically, he moved one foot awkwardly after the other. He flexed his arms, examined his body – and then, without warning, dashed off, away from the boys.

19

Peter laughed, a pure, high-pitched sound. He reached out lithely and snatched back the running clay figure. It struggled and fought frantically as he drew it close to him.

'Gosh,' Dave whispered.

Peter rolled the clay man briskly between his palms. He kneaded the soft clay together in a shapeless lump. Then he pulled it apart. Rapidly, expertly, he formed two clay figures, two little clay men half the size of the first. He set them down, and leaned calmly back to wait.

First one, then the other, stirred. They got up, tried out their arms and legs and began rapidly to move. One ran off in one direction; the other hesitated, started after his companion, then chose an opposite course past Noaks, toward the street.

'Get him!' Peter ordered sharply. He snatched up the first one, jumped quickly to his feet and hurried after the other. It ran desperately – straight toward Doctor Meade's station wagon.

As the station wagon started up, the tiny clay figure made a frantic leap. Its tiny arms groped wildly as it tried to find purchase on the smooth metal fender. Unconcerned, the station wagon moved out into traffic, and the tiny figure was left behind, still waving its arms futilely, trying to climb and catch hold of a surface already gone.

Peter caught up with it. His foot came down and the clay man was squashed into a shapeless blob of moist clay.

Walter and Dave and Noaks came slowly over; they approached in a wide, cautious circle. 'You got him?' Noaks demanded hoarsely.

'Sure,' Peter said. He was already scraping the clay off his shoe, his small face calm and smooth. 'Of course I got him. He belonged to me, didn't he?'

The boys were silent. Peter could see they were frightened. That puzzled him. What was there to be afraid of?

He started to speak to them, but at that moment the dusty yellow Packard came screeching to a stop, and he turned his attention to it, the clay figures forgotten.

The motor clicked into silence and the door opened. A man got slowly out. He was good-looking, fairly young. Black tangled hair, heavy eyebrows, white teeth. He looked tired. His gray double-breasted suit was rumpled and stained; his brown shoes were scuffed and his tie was twisted to one side. His face was lined, haggard with fatigue. His eyes were swollen and bleary. He came slowly toward the boys, focused his attention on them with an effort and said, 'Is this the boarding house?'

None of the boys answered. They could see the man was a stranger. Everybody in town knew Mrs Trilling's boarding house; this man was from somewhere else. His car had New York license plates; he was from New York. None of them had ever seen him before. And he talked with a strange accent, a rapid, clipped bark, harsh and vaguely unpleasant.

Peter stirred slightly. 'What do you want?'

'A place. A room.' The man dug in his pocket and got out a pack of cigarettes and his lighter. He lit up shakily; the cigarette almost got away from him. All this the boys saw with mild interest and faint distaste.

'I'll go tell my mother,' Peter said at last. He turned his back on the man and walked calmly toward the front porch. Without looking back he entered the cool, dim house, his steps turned toward the sounds of dish-washing coming from the big kitchen.

Mrs Trilling peered around peevishly at her son. 'What do you want? Keep out of the ice box. You can't have anything until dinner time; I told you that!'

'There's a man outside. He wants a room.' Peter added, 'He's a stranger.'

21

Mabel Trilling dried her hands quickly, swollen face suddenly animated. 'Don't just stand there! Go tell him to come in. Is he alone?'

'Just him.'

Mabel Trilling hurried past her son, outside onto the porch and down the sagging steps. The man was still there, thank God. She breathed a silent prayer of relief. People didn't seen to come through Millgate anymore. The boarding house was only half-filled: a few retired old men, the town librarian, a clerk, and her own apartment. 'What can I do for you?' she demanded breathlessly.

'I want a room,' Ted Barton answered wearily. 'Just a room. I don't care what it's like or how much it costs.'

'Do you want meals? If you eat with us you'll save fifty percent over what you'd have to pay down at the Steak House, and my meals are every bit as good as those tough little dry things they try to push off on you, especially a gentleman from out of town. You're from New York?'

An agonized twist crossed the man's face; it was quickly fought down. 'Yes, I'm from New York.'

'I hope you'll like Millgate,' Mrs Trilling rushed on, drying her hands on her apron. 'It's a quiet little town, we don't ever have any trouble of any kind. Are you in business, Mr – '

'Ted Barton.'

'You're in business, Mr Barton? I suppose you're down here for a rest. A lot of New York people leave their places in the summer, don't they? I guess it gets pretty awful up there. You don't mind telling me what line you're in, do you? Are you all by yourself? Nobody else with you?' She caught hold of his sleeve. 'Come on inside and I'll show you your room. How long did you figure to stay?'

22

Barton followed after her, up the steps and onto the porch. 'I don't know. Maybe a while. Maybe not.'

'You're alone, are you?'

'My wife may join me later if I stay here very long. I left her back in Martinsville.'

'Your business?' Mrs Trilling repeated, as they climbed the worn-carpeted stairs to the second floor.

'Insurance.'

'This is your room. Facing the hills. You'll get a nice view. Aren't the hills lovely?' She pulled aside the plain white curtains, washed many times. 'Ever seen such lovely hills in your life?'

'Yes,' Barton said. 'They're nice.' He moved aimlessly around the room, touching the shabby iron bed, the tall white dresser, the picture on the wall. 'This'll be all right. How much?'

Mrs Trilling's eyes darted craftily. 'You're going to eat with us, of course. Two meals a day, lunch and dinner.' She licked her lips. 'Forty dollars.'

Barton fumbled in his pocket for his wallet. He didn't seem to care. He peeled some bills from his wallet and handed them to her without a word.

'Thank you,' Mrs Trilling breathed. She backed quickly out of the room. 'Dinner's at seven. You missed lunch, but if you want I can – '

'No.' Barton shook his head. 'That's all. I don't want any lunch.' He turned his back on her and gazed moodily out the window.

Her footsteps died down the hall. Barton lit a cigarette. He felt vaguely sick at his stomach and his head ached from the driving. After leaving Peg at the hotel in Martinsville, he had sped back here. He had to come back. He had to stay here, even if it took years. He had to

23

find out who he was, and this was the only place there was any chance of learning.

Barton smiled ironically. Even here, there didn't seem to be much of a chance. A boy had died of scarlet fever eighteen years ago. Nobody remembered. A minor incident; hundreds of kids died, people came and went. One death, one name out of many . . .

The door of the room opened.

Barton turned quickly. A boy stood there, small and thin, with immense brown eyes. With a start, Barton recognized him as the landlady's son. 'What do you want?' he demanded. 'What's the idea of coming in here?'

The boy closed the door after him. For a moment he hesitated, then abruptly asked, 'Who are you?'

Barton stiffened. 'Barton. Ted Barton.'

The boy seemed satisfied. He walked all around Barton, examining him from every side. 'How did you get through?' he demanded. 'Most people don't get through. There must be a reason.'

'Through?' Barton was puzzled. 'Through what?'

'Through the barrier.' Suddenly the boy withdrew; his eyes filmed over. Barton realized the boy had let something slip, something he hadn't meant to tell.

'What barrier? Where?'

The boy shrugged. 'The mountains. It's a long way. The road's bad. Why did you come here? What are you doing?'

It might have been just childish curiosity. Or was it more? The boy was odd-looking, thin and bony, with huge eyes, a shock of brown hair over his unusually wide forehead. An intelligent face. Sensitive for a boy living in an out-of-the-way town in southeastern Virginia.

'Maybe,' Barton said slowly, 'I have ways to get past the barrier.'

The reaction came quickly. The boy's body tensed; his eyes lost their dull film and began to glint nervously. He moved back, away from Barton, uneasy and suddenly shaken. 'Oh yeah?' he muttered. But his voice lacked conviction. 'What sort of ways? You must have crawled through a weak place.'

'I drove down the road. The main highway.'

The huge brown eyes flickered. 'Sometimes the barrier isn't there. You must have come through when it wasn't there.'

Now Barton was beginning to feel uneasy. He was bluffing, and his bluff had been called. The boy knew what the barrier was, but Barton didn't. A tinge of fear licked at him. Come to think of it, he *hadn't* seen any other cars either coming or going from Millgate; the road was run-down and almost unusable. Weeds covered it; the surface was dry and cracked. No traffic at all. Hills and fields, sagging fences. Maybe he could learn something from this boy.

'How long,' he asked cautiously, 'have you known about the barrier?'

The boy shrugged. 'What do you mean? I've always known about it.'

'Does everybody else here know about it?'

The boy laughed. 'Of course not. If they knew – ' He broke off, the veil again slipping over his huge brown eyes. Barton had lost his momentary advantage; the boy was on safe ground again, answering questions instead of asking. He knew more than Barton, and they both realized it.

'You're a pretty smart kid,' Barton said. 'How old are you?'

'Ten.'

'What's your name?'

'Peter.'

'You've always lived here? In Millgate?'

'Sure.' His small chest swelled. 'Where else?'

Barton hesitated. 'Have you ever been outside of town? On the other side of the barrier?'

The boy frowned. His face struggled; Barton sensed he had hit on something. Peter began to pace restlessly around the room, hands in the pockets of his faded blue jeans. 'Sure. Lots of times.'

'How do you get across?'

'I have ways.'

'Let's compare ways,' Barton said promptly. But there was no bite; his gambit was warily declined.

'Let's see your watch,' the boy asked. 'How many jewels does it have?'

Barton removed his wristwatch cautiously and passed it over. 'Twenty-one jewels.'

'It's nice.' Peter turned it over and around. He ran his delicate fingers over the surface, then passed it back. 'Does everybody in New York have a watch like that?'

'Everybody who is anybody.'

After a moment Peter said, 'I can stop time. Not very long – maybe four hours. Someday it'll be a whole day. What do you think of that?'

Bartin didn't know what to think. 'What else can you do?' he said warily. 'That's not much.'

'I have power over *its* creatures.'

'Whose?'

Peter shrugged. 'It. You know. The one on this side. With the hands stuck out. Not the one with the bright hair, like metal. The other one. Didn't you see it?'

Barton hazarded, 'No, I didn't.'

Peter was puzzled. 'You *must* have seen it. You must

26

have seen both of them. They're there all the time. Sometimes I go up the road and sit on a ledge I have. Where I can see them good.'

After a pause, Barton managed to find words. 'Maybe you'll take me along some time.'

'It's nice.' The boy's cheeks flushed; in his enthusiasm he lost his suspicion. 'On a clear day you can see both of them easily. Especially him – at the far end.' He began to giggle. 'It's a funny thing. At first it gave me the willies. But I got used to it.'

'Do you know their names?' Barton asked tautly, trying to find some thread of reason, some sanity in the boy's words. 'Who are they?'

'I don't know.' Peter's flush deepened. 'But some time I'm going to find out. There must be a way. I've asked some of the first-level things, but they don't know. I even made up a special golem with an extra-large brain, but it couldn't tell me anything. Maybe you can help me with that. How are you on the clay? Are you experienced?' He came close to Barton and lowered his voice. 'Nobody around here knows *anything*. There's actual opposition. I have to work completely alone. If I had some help . . .'

'Yeah,' Barton managed. Good Lord, what had he got himself into?

'I'd like to trace one of the Wanderers,' Peter continued, with a rush of excitement. 'See where they come from and how they do it. If I had help maybe I could learn to do it, too.'

Barton was paralyzed. What were Wanderers and what did they do? 'Yeah, when the two of us work together,' he began weakly, but Peter cut him off.

'Let's see your hand.' Peter took hold of Barton's wrist and examined his palm carefully. Abruptly he backed away. The color died from his cheeks. 'You were lying!

27

You don't know anything!' Panic flashed across his face. 'You don't know anything at all!'

'Sure, I do,' Barton asserted. But there was no conviction. And on the boy's face the surprise and fear had turned to dull disgust and hostility. Peter turned and pulled open the hall door.

'You don't know anything,' he repeated, half in anger, half with contempt. He paused briefly. 'But I know something.'

'What sort of thing?' Barton demanded. He was going the whole way; it was too late to pull back now.

'Something you don't know.' A veiled, secretive smile flitted across the smooth young face. An evasive, cunning expression.

'What is it?' Barton demanded hoarsely. 'What do you know that I don't know?'

He didn't expect the answer he got. And before he could react, the door had shut with a bang, and the boy was racing off down the corridor. Barton stood unmoving, hearing the echoing clatter of heels against the worn steps.

The boy ran outside, onto the porch. Under Barton's window, he cupped his hands and shouted at the top of his lungs. Dimly, a faint, penetrating yell that broke against Barton's ears, a shattering repetition of the same words, spoken in exactly the same way.

'I know who you are,' the words came again, lapping harshly against him. 'I know who you *really* are!'

# FOUR

Certain that the man wasn't following him, and mildly satisfied with the effect of his words, Peter Trilling made his way through the rubble and debris behind the house. He passed the pig pens, opened the gate to the back field, closed it carefully after him, and headed toward the barn.

The barn smelled of hay and manure. It was hot; the air was stale and dead, a vast blanket of buzzing afternoon heat. He climbed the ladder cautiously, one eye on the blazing doorway; there was still a chance the man had followed him.

On the loft, he perched expertly and waited a time, getting his breath and going over what had happened.

He had made a mistake. A bad mistake. The man had learned plenty and *he* hadn't learned anything. At least, he hadn't learned *much*. The man was an enigma in many ways. He'd have to be careful, watch his step and go slow. But the man might turn out to be valuable.

Peter got to his feet and found the flashlight hanging from its rusty nail above his head, where two huge beams crossed. Its yellow light cut a patch into the depths of the loft.

They were still there, exactly as he had left them. Nobody ever came here; it was his work chamber. He sat down on the moldy hay and laid the light beside him. Then he reached out and carefully lifted the first cage.

The rat's eyes glittered, red and tiny in its thick pelt of

matted gray fur. It shifted and pulled away, as he slid aside the door of the cage and reached in for it.

'Come on,' he whispered. 'Don't be afraid.'

He drew the rat out and held its quivering body in his hands while he stroked its fur. The long whiskers twitched; the never-ceasing movements of its nose grew, as it sniffed his fingers and sleeve.

'Nothing to eat right now,' he said to it. 'I just want to see how big you're getting.' He pushed the rat back into its cage and closed the wire door. Then he turned the light from one cage to the next, on each of the quivering gray forms that huddled against the wire, eyes red, noses moving constantly. They were all there. All in good shape. Fat and healthy. Back into the depths, row after row. Heaped and stacked and piled on each other.

He got up and examined the spider jars arranged in even, precise rows on the overhead shelves. The insides of the jars were thick with webs, tangled heaps like the hair of old women. He could see the spiders moving sluggishly, dulled by the heat. Fat globes that reflected the beam of the flashlight. He dipped into the moth-box and got out a handful of little dead bodies. Expertly, he fed each jar, careful that none escaped.

Everything was fine. He clicked off the flashlight, hung it back up, paused for a moment to study the blazing doorway, and then crept back down the ladder.

At the workbench he picked up a pair of pliers and continued on the glass-windowed snake box. It was coming along pretty well, considering it was his first. Later on, when he had more experience, he wouldn't take so long.

He measured the frame and computed the size glass he would need. Where could he find a window no one would miss? Maybe the smoke house; it had been abandoned

30

since the roof began to leak early last spring. He put down his pencil, grabbed up the yardstick, and hurried out of the barn, into the bright sunlight.

As he raced across the field, his heart thumped with excitement. Things were coming along fine. Slowly, surely, he was gaining an edge. Of course, this man might upset everything. He'd have to make sure his weight wasn't thrown on the wrong side of the Scale. How much that weight would count for, there was no way to tell yet. Offhand, he'd guess very little.

But what was he doing in Millgate? Vague tendrils of doubt plucked at the boy's mind. He had come for a reason. Ted Barton. He'd have to make inquiries. If necessary, the man could be neutralized. But it might be possible to get him on the –

Something buzzed. Peter shrieked and threw himself to one side. A blinding pain stabbed through his neck, another seared across his arm. He rolled over and over on the hot grass, screaming and flailing his arms. Waves of terror beat at him; he tried desperately to bury himself in the hard soil.

The buzz faded. It ceased. There was only the sound of the wind. He was alone.

Trembling with terror, Peter raised his head and opened his eyes. His whole body shuddered; shock waves rolled up and down him. His arm and neck burned horribly; they'd got him in two places.

But thank God they were on their own. Unorganized.

He got unsteadily to his feet. No others. He cursed wildly; what a fool he was to come blundering out in the open this way. Suppose a whole pack had found him, not just two!

He forgot about the window and headed back toward the barn. A close call. Maybe next time he wouldn't get off so easy. And the two had got away; he hadn't managed to crush them. They'd carry word back; she'd know. She'd have something to gloat about. An easy victory. She'd get pleasure out of it.

He was gaining the edge, but it wasn't safe, not yet. He still had to be careful. He could overplay his hand, lose everything he'd built up in a single second. Pull the whole thing down around him.

And worse – send the Scales tipping back, a clatter of falling dominos all along the line. It was so inter-woven . . .

He began searching for some mud to put on the bee stings.


'What's the matter, Mr Barton?' a genial voice asked, close to his ear. 'Sinus trouble? Most people who hold onto their noses like that have sinus trouble.'

Barton roused himself. He had almost fallen asleep over his dinner plate. His coffee had cooled to a scummy brown; the greasy potatoes were hardening fast. 'Beg pardon?' he muttered.

The man sitting next to him pushed his chair back and wiped his mouth with his napkin. He was plump and well-dressed; a middle-aged man in a dark blue pin-striped suit and white shirt, attractive tie, heavy ring on his thick white finger. 'My name's Meade. Ernest Meade. The way you hold your head.' He smiled a gold-toothed profes-sional smile. 'I'm a doctor. Maybe I can help.'

'Just tired,' Barton said.

'You just arrived here, didn't you? This is a good place. I eat here once in a while when I'm too lazy to cook my own meals. Mrs Trilling doesn't mind serving me, do you, Mrs T?'

At the far end of the table, Mrs Trilling nodded in

vague agreement. Her face was less swollen; with nightfall the pollen didn't carry as far. Most of the other boarders had left their places and gone out on the screened-in porch to sit in the cool darkness until bedtime.

'What brings you to Millgate, Mr Barton?' the doctor asked politely. He fumbled in his coat pocket and got out a brown cigar. 'Not very many people come this way anymore. It's a strange thing. We used to get a lot of traffic, but now it's died to nothing. Come to think of it, you're about the first new face I've seen in quite a spell.'

Barton digested this information. A flicker of interest warmed him. Meade was a doctor. Maybe he knew something. Barton finished his coffee and asked cautiously, 'Have you been practicing here long, doctor?'

'All my life.' Meade made a faint gesture with his thumb. 'I have a private hospital at the top of the rise. Shady House, it's called.' He lowered his voice. 'The town doesn't provide any sort of decent medical care. I try to help out as best I can; built my own hospital and operate it at my own expense.'

Barton chose his words carefully. 'There were some relatives of mine living here. A long time ago.'

'Barton?' Meade reflected. 'How long ago?'

'Eighteen or twenty years ago.' Watching the doctor's florid, competent face, Barton continued, 'Donald and Sarah Barton. They had a son. Born in 1926.'

'A son?' Meade looked interested. 'Seems to me I recall something. '26? I probably brought him into this world. I was practicing then. Of course, I was a lot younger in those days. But weren't we all.'

'The boy died,' Barton said slowly. 'He died in 1935. From scarlet fever. A contaminated water hole.'

The florid face twisted. 'By God. I remember that. Why, I had that closed; it was my idea. I forced them to

33

close it. Those were relatives of yours? That boy was related to you?' He puffed on his cigar angrily. 'I remember that. Three or four kids died by the time it was over. The kid's name was Barton? Seems to me I recall. Related to you, you say?' He culled his brain. 'There was one kid. Sweet boy. Dark hair like yours. Same general physiognomy. Come to think of it, I knew you reminded me of someone.'

Barton's breath caught. 'You remember him?' He leaned toward the doctor. '*You actually saw him die?*'

'I saw them all die. That was before Shady House was built. Sure, at the old county hospital. Christ, what a pest hole. No wonder they died. Filthy, incompetent; it was on account of that I built my own place.' He shook his head. 'We could have saved them all, these days. Easily. But it's too late now.' He touched Barton briefly on the arm. 'I'm sorry. But you couldn't have been very old then, yourself. What relation were you to the boy?'

A good question, Barton thought to himself. He would have liked to know the answer, too.

'Come to think of it,' Doctor Meade said slowly, half to himself, 'seems to me that child's name was the same as yours. Isn't your Christian name Theodore?'

Barton nodded. 'That's right.'

The florid brown wrinkled, perplexed. 'The same as yours. I knew I'd heard the name, when Mrs Trilling told me.'

Barton's hands clenched around the edge of the table. 'Doctor, is he buried here in town? Is his grave around here?'

Meade nodded slowly. 'Sure. In the regular city cemetery.' He shot Barton a shrewd glance. 'You want to visit? No trouble to do that. Is that what you came here for? To visit his grave?'

'Not exactly,' Barton answered woodenly.

At the end of the table, beside his mother, sat Peter Trilling. His neck was swollen and angry. His right arm was bandaged with a strip of dirty gauze. He looked sullen and unhappy. An accident? Had something bitten him? Barton watched the boy's thin fingers pluck at a piece of bread. *I know who you are,* the boy had shouted. *I know who you really are.* Did he know or was it just a boy's boast? A conceited threat, empty and meaningless?

'Look here,' Doctor Meade said. 'I don't mean to pry into your affairs; that's not right. But there's something bothering you. You didn't come here for a rest.'

'That's right,' Barton said.

'You want to tell me what it is? I'm a lot older than you. And I've lived in this town a long time. I was born here, grew up here. I know everybody around here. Brought a lot of them into this world.'

Was this a person he could talk to? A possible friend? 'Doctor,' Barton said slowly, 'that boy who died was related to me. But I don't know how.' He rubbed his forehead wearily. 'I don't understand it. I've got to find out what I am to that boy.'

'Why?'

'I can't tell you that.'

The doctor got out a silver toothpick from a little engraved box and began thoughtfully to pick at his molars. 'Did you go down to the newspaper office? Nat Tate'll give you some help. Old records, pictures, newspapers. And at the police station you can go over a lot of city records. Taxes and duns and assessments and fines. Of course, if you're trying to trace a family relationship, the best thing is the county courthouse.'

'What I want is here in Millgate. Not at the county courthouse.' After a moment Barton added, 'It has to do with the whole town. Not just Ted Barton. I have to know about all of this.' He moved his hand in a tired circle. 'It's all involved, somehow. Tied in with Ted Barton. The other Ted Barton, I mean.'

Doctor Meade considered. Abruptly he put his silver toothpick away and got to his feet. 'Come on out on the porch. You haven't met Miss James, have you?'

Something plucked at Barton. His weariness fled and he glanced quickly up. 'I know that name. I've heard it before.'

Doctor Meade was watching him oddly. 'Probably,' he agreed. 'She was sitting across from us during dinner.' He held the porch door open. 'She's the librarian over at the Free Library. She knows all about Millgate.'

The porch was dark. It took a couple of minutes for Barton to get adjusted. Several shapes were sitting around on old-fashioned chairs and a long sagging couch. Smoking, dozing, enjoying the evening coolness. The porch was protected by wire screens; no insects had got in to immolate themselves on the single electric bulb glowing faintly in the corner.

'Miss James,' Doctor Meade said, 'this is Ted Barton. Maybe you can help him. He has a few problems.'

Miss James smiled up at Barton through her thick, rimless glasses. 'I'm glad to meet you,' she said in a soft voice. 'You're new around here, aren't you?'

Barton seated himself on the arm of the couch. 'I'm from New York,' he answered.

'You're the first person through here in years,' Doctor Meade observed. He blew a vast cloud of cigar smoke around the dark porch. The red glow of his cigar lit up the gloom. 'The road's practically ready to fall apart. Nobody comes this way. We see the same old faces month after month. But we have our work. I have the hospital. I like

36

to learn new things, experiment, work with my patients. I have about ten fairly dependent people up there. Once in a while we get in a few of the town wives to help. Right now it's pretty quiet.'

'Do you know anything about a – barrier?' Barton asked Miss James abruptly.

'A barrier?' Doctor Meade demanded. 'What kind of a barrier?'

'You've never heard of it?'

Doctor Meade shook his head slowly. 'No, not that I can think of.'

'I, neither,' Miss James echoed. 'In what connection?'

No one else was listening. The others were dozing and murmuring together at the far end of the porch. Mrs Trilling, the other boarders, Peter, Doctor Meade's daughter Mary, some neighbors. 'What do you know about the Trilling boy?' Barton asked.

Meade grunted. 'Seems to be healthy enough.'

'Have you ever examined him?'

'Of course,' Meade answered, annoyed. 'I've examined everybody in this town. He has a high IQ; seems to be alert. Plays a lot by himself.' He added, 'Frankly, I never liked precocious children.'

'But he's not interested in books,' Miss James protested. 'He never comes to the library.'

Barton was silent for a time. Then he asked, 'What would it mean if somebody said, "The one on the far side. The one with his hands out." Does that mean anything to you?'

Miss James and Doctor Meade were baffled. 'Sounds like a game,' Doctor Meade muttered.

'No,' Barton answered. 'Not a game.' And he meant it. 'Let it go. Forget I said anything.'

Miss James leaned toward him. 'Mr Barton, I may be

37

wrong, but I receive the distinct impression that you think there's something here. Something very important here in Millgate. Am I right?'

Barton's lips twisted. 'There's something going on. Beyond human awareness.'

'Here? In Millgate?'

Words forced their way between Barton's lips. 'I've got to find out. I can't go on like this. Somebody in this town must know. You can't all sit around and pretend everything is perfectly ordinary! Somebody in this town knows the real story.'

'Story about what?' Meade rumbled, perplexed.

'*About me.*'

They were both agitated. 'How do you mean?' Miss James faltered. 'Is there somebody here who knows you?'

'There's somebody here who knows everything. The *why* and *how*. Something I don't understand. Something ominous and alien. And you all sit around and enjoy yourselves.' He got abruptly to his feet. 'I'm sorry. I'm exhausted. I'll see you later.'

'Where are you going?' Meade demanded.

'Up to my room. To get some sleep.'

'Look here, Barton. I'll give you a few phenobarbitals. They'll help calm you. And if you want, drop up to the hospital tomorrow. I'll give you a check-up. Seems to me you're under a hell of a strain. In a young man like you that's somewhat – '

'Mr Barton,' Miss James said softly, but insistently, with a fixed smile on her face, 'I assure you there's nothing strange about Millgate. I wish there were. It's the most ordinary town you could find. If I thought there was anything going on here of any interest whatsoever, I'd be the first to want to learn more.'

Barton opened his mouth to answer. But the words

38

never came. They were bitten off, lost forever. What he saw made even the memory of them dissolve into nothingness.

Two shapes, faintly luminous, emerged from one end of the porch. A man and a woman, walking together, holding hands. They appeared to be talking, but no sound came. They moved silently, calmly, across the porch, toward the opposite wall. They passed within a foot of Barton; he could see their faces clearly. They were young. The woman had long blonde hair, heavy twisted braids that fell down her neck and shoulders. A thin, sharp face. Pale skin, smooth and perfect. Exquisite lips and teeth. And the young man beside her was equally handsome.

Neither of them noticed Barton or the boarders sitting on their chairs. Their eyes were shut tight. They passed through the chairs, the couch, through the reclining boarders. Through Doctor Meade and Miss James, and then through the far wall. Abruptly, they were gone. The two half-luminous shapes had vanished as quickly as they had come. Without a sound.

'Good God,' Barton managed at last. 'Did you see them?' No one had stirred. Some of the boarders had stopped their conversation momentarily, but now they resumed their low murmurs as if nothing had happened. 'Did you see them?' he demanded excitedly.

Miss James seemed puzzled. 'Of course,' she murmured. 'We all saw them. They come through here about this time each evening. They're taking a walk. A nice couple, don't you think?'

'But – who – what – ' Barton gasped.

'Is this the first time you've seen Wanderers?' Meade asked. His calm was suddenly shaken. 'You mean you don't have Wanderers where you come from?'

'No,' Barton said. Everyone was watching him in

amazement. 'What are they? They walked *through* the walls. Through the furniture. Through you!'

'Of course,' Miss James said primly. 'That's why they're called Wanderers. They can go anywhere. Through anything. Didn't you know that?'

'How long has it been going on?' Barton demanded.

The answer didn't really surprise him. But the calmness of it did. 'Always,' Miss James said. 'As long as I can recall.'

'Seems to me there've always been Wanderers,' Doctor Meade agreed, puffing on his cigar. 'But it's perfectly natural. What's so strange about that?'

# FIVE

The morning was warm and sunny. The dew hadn't been baked off the weeds yet. The sky was a mild, hazy blue, not yet heated up to blazing incandescence. That would come later, as the sun climbed toward its zenith. A faint breeze stirred the cedars that grew in a line along the slope behind the immense stone building. The cedars cast pools of shade; they were responsible for the name Shady House.

Shady House overlooked the town proper. A single road twisted up the rise to the flat surface where the building stretched out. The grounds were carefully tended. Flowers and trees, and a long wood fence that formed a protecting square. Patients could be seen lounging around, sitting on benches, chairs, even stretched out on the warm ground, resting. There was an air of peace and quietude about the hospital. Some place in its depths Doctor Meade was working. Probably down in his littered office, with his microscope and slides and x-rays and chemicals.

Mary crouched in a concealed hollow, just beyond the line of towering cedars. The hard soil had been scooped out by shovels when Shady House was built. Where she sat she couldn't be seen by anyone at the House. The cedars and the wall of rock and earth cut the view off sharply. Spread out beneath her, and around her on three sides, was the valley. And beyond that, the eternal ring of mountains, blue and green, tipped with faint hazy white. Silent and unmoving.

'Go on,' Mary said. She shifted a little, tucked her slim legs under her, and made herself more comfortable. She was listening intently, trying not to miss a single word.

'It was pure chance,' the bee continued. Its voice was thin and faint, almost lost in the stirring early-morning breeze that rustled through the cedars. It was perched on the leaf of a flower, close to the girl's ear. 'We happened to be scouting in that area. No one saw him go in. All at once he came out, and we dived on him. I wish there had been more of us; he doesn't often come so far this way. He was actually over the line.'

Mary was deep in thought. The sunlight glinted on her black hair, shiny and heavy around her neck. Her dark eyes sparkled as she asked. 'Have you been able to tell what he's doing in there?'

'Not very well. He's set up some kind of interference around the whole place. We can't get close. Have to depend on secondary information. Unreliable, as you know.'

'You think he's assembling defensive units? Or – '

'Or worse. He may be nearing some kind of overt stage. He's built a lot of containers. Of various sizes. There's a certain irony in this. The scouts we've sent in have died in the interference zone. He's collected their corpses every day and used them for feed. This amuses him.'

Automatically, Mary reached out her small shoe and crushed a black grass-spider that was hurrying by. 'I know,' she said slowly. 'After I left the game yesterday, he golemed the clay I was using. That's a bad sign. He must feel he's gaining or he wouldn't try it on my clay. He knows the risk. Clay gathered by others is unstable. And I must have left some kind of imprint.'

'It's probably true that he has a minor advantage,' the bee answered. 'He's a tireless worker. Nevertheless, he displayed overt fear when we attacked him. He's still vulnerable. And he knows it.'

Mary pulled a blade of grass loose and thoughtfully chewed it between her white teeth. 'Both his figures attempted to escape. One came very close. It ran directly toward me, in the station wagon. But I didn't dare stop.'

'Who is this man?' the bee asked. 'This person from outside. It's unique, someone coming through the barrier. You think he might be imitation? Something projected out, then brought in to appear as an external factor? So far, he doesn't really seem to have made any difference.'

Mary raised her dark eyes. 'No, not so far. But I think he will.'

'Really?'

'I'm fairly sure. If – '

'If what?' The bee was interested.

Mary ignored it; she was deep in thought. 'He's in a curious situation,' she murmured. 'He's already faced with the fact that his memories don't agree with the situation.'

'They don't?'

'Of course not. He's become aware of major discrepancies. Essentially, he remembers a completely different town, with totally different people.' She killed another small spider that was moving cautiously up. For a time she studied its inert body. 'And he's the kind of person who won't be satisfied until he understands the situation.'

'He makes things confusing,' the bee complained.

'For whom? For me?' Mary got up slowly and brushed grass from her jeans. 'For Peter, perhaps. He's made so many careful plans.'

The bee flew up from its leaf and landed on the girl's collar. 'Perhaps he'll try to learn something from this man.'

Mary laughed. 'He'd like to, of course. But there's not much the man can tell him. He's so confused and uncertain.'

'Peter will try. He's tireless, the way he explores every possibility for knowledge. Almost like a bee.'

Mary agreed, as she walked back up the slope toward the cedars. 'Yes, he's tireless, but a little too confident. He may wind up by doing himself more harm than good. In trying to find out things he may reveal more than he learns. The man, I think, is clever. And he *must* find out about himself. He'll probably come out ahead; that's been the pattern, so far.'

Barton made sure no one was around. He stood close to the old-fashioned telephone, turned so he could look up and down the hall, at all the doors and the stairs at the far end, and then dropped a dime into the coin slot.

'Number please,' the tinny voice said in his ear.

He asked for the Calhoun Hotel in Martinsville. After three more dimes and a series of clicks and waits, there was a distant buzzing.

'Calhoun Hotel,' a far-off voice came, a man's sleepy drawl.

'Let me talk to Mrs Barton. In 204.'

Another pause. More clicks. Then –

'Ted!' Peg's voice, wild with impatience and alarm. 'Is that you?'

'It's me. I suppose.'

'Where *are* you? In the name of heaven, are you going to just leave me here in this awful hotel?' Her voice rose in shrill hysteria. 'Ted, I've had enough. I can't stand it anymore. You've got the car; I can't do anything, go anywhere, and you're acting like a crazy person!'

Barton spoke close to the phone, voice muted. 'I tried

to explain it to you. This town. It's not what I remember. My mind's been tampered with, I think. Something I found in the newspaper office makes me sure even my identity isn't – '

'Good God,' Peg cut in. 'We haven't got time to waste looking up your childhood illusions! How long are you going to keep this up?'

'I don't know,' Barton answered helplessly. 'There's so much I don't understand. If I knew more I'd tell you.'

There was a moment of silence. 'Ted,' Peg said, with hard calm, 'if you don't come back and get me in the next twenty-four hours, I'm leaving. I have enough money to get back up to Washington. You know I've got friends there. You won't see me again, except perhaps in court.'

'Are you serious?'

'Yes.'

Barton licked his lips. 'Peg, I've got to stay here. I've learned a few things, not much, but a little. Enough to tell me I'm on the right track. If I stay here long enough I'll be able to crack this. Forces are operating here, powers that don't seem bound by – '

There was a sharp click. Peg had hung up.

Barton placed the receiver back on its hook. His mind was blank. He moved aimlessly away from the phone, hands in his pockets. Well, that was that. She meant it, every damn word. He'd show up in Martinsville, and she wouldn't be there.

A small shape detached itself from behind a table and potted fern. 'Hello,' Peter said calmly. He played with a clump of squirming things, black lumps that crawled up his wrist and over his hands.

'What's that?' Barton demanded, sickened.

'These?' Peter blinked. 'Spiders.' He captured them

45

and thrust them into his pocket. 'Are you going driving? I thought maybe I could ride in your car with you.'

The boy had been there all the time. Hidden behind the fern. Strange, he hadn't seen him; he had passed by the fern on his way to the phone. 'Why?' Barton demanded bluntly.

The boy fidgeted. His smooth face twisted hopefully. 'I've decided to let you see my ledge.'

'Oh?' Barton tried to look indifferent, but inside, his pulse rate abruptly changed. Maybe he'd learn something. 'It might be arranged.' Barton said. 'How far is it?'

'Not far.' Peter hurried to the front door and pushed it open. 'I'll show you the way.'

Barton followed slowly after him. The front porch was deserted. Empty chairs and couches, drab and terribly old. It gave him an uneasy chill; the two Wanderers had come through here last night. He touched the wall of the porch experimentally. Solid. Yet, the two youthful figures had passed calmly through, and through the chairs and reclining boarders.

Could they pass through *him*?

'Come on!' Peter shouted. He stood by the dusty yellow Packard, tugging impatiently at the door handle.

Barton got behind the wheel and the boy slid quickly in beside him. As he turned on the motor he found the boy carefully examining the corners of the car, lifting the seat cushions, squatting down on the floor and peering under the front seat.

'What are you looking for?' Barton demanded.

'Bees.' Peter emerged breathlessly. 'Can we keep the windows rolled up? They try to fly in, along the way.'

Barton released the brake, and the car glided out onto the main street. 'What's wrong with bees? You afraid of them? You're not afraid of spiders.'

46

Peter touched his still-swollen neck by way of an answer. 'Turn to the right,' he ordered. He leaned back contentedly, feet out, hands in his pockets. 'Make a complete circle up Jefferson and head back the other way.'

The ledge provided a vast panoramic view of the valley and the hills that ringed it on all sides. Barton seated himself on the rocky ground and got out his pack of cigarettes. He took a deep lungful of the warm midday air. The ledge was partly shaded by bushes and shrubs. Cool and quiet with the valley spread out below. The sun shone down through the thick blanket of blue haze that collected around the distant peaks. Nothing stirred. The fields, farms, roads and houses, all were utterly motionless.

Peter squatted beside him. 'Nice, isn't it?'

'I guess so.'

'What were you and Doctor Meade talking about last night? I couldn't hear.'

'Maybe it was none of your business.'

The boy flushed and his lips set in a sullen line. 'I can't stand him and his smelly cigars. And his silver toothpick.' He got out some of his spiders from his pocket and let them run over his hands and down his sleeves. Barton moved a little way off and tried to ignore it.

After a moment Peter asked, 'Can I have a cigarette?'

'No.'

The boy's face fell. 'All right for you.' But he brightened almost at once. 'What did you think of the two Wanderers last night? Weren't they something?'

'Oh, I don't know,' Barton answered casually. 'You see them fairly often.'

'I'd sure like to know how they do it,' Peter said feelingly. Abruptly he regretted expressing his emotions.

47

He gathered his spiders up and tossed them down the slope. They scrambled off excitedly and he pretended to watch them.

A thought struck Barton. 'Aren't you afraid of bees, out here? If one flew after you, there wouldn't be any place to hide.'

Peter laughed with regained contempt. 'Bees don't come here. It's too far in.'

'*In?*'

'In fact,' Peter continued, with cutting superiority, 'this is just about the safest place in the world.'

Barton couldn't make anything out of the boy's words. After a period of silence he observed cautiously, 'The haze is pretty thick, today.'

'The what?'

'The haze.' Barton indicated the pools of silent blue obscuring the far peaks. 'It's from the heat.'

Peter's face managed to show even more contempt. 'That's not haze. That's *him*!'

'Oh?' Barton tensed. Maybe he was finally going to learn something – if he played it careful. 'Who do you mean?'

Peter pointed. 'Don't you see him? He's sure big. Just about the biggest there is. And old. He's older than everything else put together. Even older than the world.'

Barton saw nothing. Only haze, mountains, the blue sky. Peter dug in his pocket and got out what looked like a cheap nickel-plated magnifying glass. He handed it to Barton. Barton turned it around foolishly; he started to give it back, but Peter stopped him. 'Look through it! At the mountains!'

Barton looked. And saw it. The glass was a lens-filter of some kind. It cut the haze, made it clear and sharp.

He had figured it out wrong. He had expected him to be

48

part of the scene. He *was* the scene. He was the whole far side of the world, the edge of the valley, the mountains, the sky, everything. The whole distant rim of the universe swept up in a massive column, a cosmic tower of being, which gained shape and substance as he focused the filter-lens.

It was a man, all right. His feet were planted on the floor of the valley; the valley became his feet at the farthest edge. His legs were the mountains – or the mountains were his legs; Barton couldn't tell which. Two columns, spread apart, wide and solid. Firmly planted and balanced. His body was the mass of blue-gray haze, or what he had thought was haze. Where the mountains joined the sky, the immense torso of the man came into being.

He had his arms out over the valley. Poised above it, above the distant half. His hands were held above it in an opaque curtain, which Barton had mistaken for a layer of dust and haze. The massive figure was bent slightly forward. As if leaning intently over his part, his half of the valley. He was gazing down; his face was obscured. He didn't move. He was utterly motionless.

Motionless, but he was alive. Not a stone image, a frozen statue. He was alive, but he was outside of time. There was no change, no motion for him. He was eternal. The averted head was the most striking part of him. It seemed to glow, a clearly radiant orb, pulsing with life and brilliance.

His head was the sun.

'What's his name?' Barton asked, after a while. Now that he saw the figure, he couldn't lose it. Like one of those games – as soon as the hidden shape becomes visible it's impossible not to see it.

'I told you I don't know his name,' Peter retorted

peevishly. 'Maybe she knows. She probably knows both their names. If I knew his name I'd have power over him. I'd sure like to. He's the one I don't like. This one doesn't bother me at all. That's why I have my ledge on this side.'

'This one?' Barton echoed, puzzled. He twisted his neck and looked straight up, through the tiny circle of glass.

It made him feel somewhat strange to realize that he was part of this one. As the other figure was the distant side of the valley, this figure was the near side. And Barton was sitting on this side.

The figure rose around him. He couldn't exactly see it; he could sense it vaguely and no more. It flowed up on all sides of him. From the rocks, the fields, the tumbled heaps of shrubs and vines. This one, also, formed itself from the valley and mountains, the sky and haze. But it didn't glow. He couldn't see its head, its final dimensions. A cold chill moved through him. He had a distinct, sharp intuition. This one didn't culminate in the bright orb of the sun. This one culminated in something else.

In darkness?

He got unsteadily to his feet. 'That's enough for me. I'm going.' He began to make his way down the side of the hill. Well, he had asked for it. He was still holding numbly onto Peter's magnifying glass; he tossed it up on the ledge and continued toward the floor of the valley.

No matter where he was, no matter where he sat or stood or slept or walked, as long as he was in the valley, he was part of one or the other figure. Each made up one side of the valley, one hemisphere. He could move from one to the other, but he was always in one of them. In the center of the valley was a line. On the other side of that line he would merge with the other figure.

'Where are you going?' Peter shouted.

'Out.'

Peter's face darkened ominously. 'You can't go out. You can't leave.'

'Why not?'

'You'll find out why not.'

Barton ignored him and continued picking his way down the hill, toward the road and his parked car.

# SIX

He headed the Packard up the road, away from Millgate. Cedars and pines grew in massive profusion above and below him. The road was a narrow ribbon gouged through the forest. It was in bad shape. He drove cautiously, taking in the details. The surface of the pavement was cracked, interlaced lines and splits. Weeds jutted up. Weeds and dry grass. Nobody came along here. That much was clear.

He turned a sharp curve and abruptly slammed on the brakes. The car screeched to a halt, tires sizzling.

There it was. Spread across the road ahead of him. The sight completely floored him. He had gone along this road three times – once out and twice in – and seen nothing. Now, here it was. It had finally showed up, just as he had made up his mind to leave and forget the whole thing, join Peg and try to continue his vacation as if nothing had happened.

He would have expected something weird. Something vast and macabre, an ominous wall of some sort, mysterious and cosmic. A supraterrestrial layer barring the road.

But he was wrong. It was a stalled lumber truck. An ancient truck, with iron wheels and no gear shift. Round headlights, the old-fashioned brass lamps. Its load was spilled all the way across the highway. The wires had broken; the truck had careened at an angle and stopped dead, logs spilling off in all directions.

Barton climbed wearily out of the car. Everything was

silent. Somewhere, far off, a crow squawked dismally. The cedars rustled. He approached the sea of logs, with it archaic island jutting up in the center. Not bad, for a barrier. No car could get through that. Logs were everywhere and they were plenty big. Some were heaped on others. A dangerous, unsteady mass of twisted beams, ready to spill and roll any moment. And the road was steep.

There was no one in the truck, of course. God knew how long it had been there, or how often. Apparently, it was selective. He lit a cigarette and took off his coat; the day was starting to heat up. How would he go about getting past it? He had got by before, but this time it wasn't going to cooperate.

Maybe he could go around.

The high side was out of the question. He'd never be able to scramble up the almost perpendicular bank, and if he lost his grip on the smooth rock, he'd pitch down into the twisted mass of logs. Maybe the low side. Between the road and the slope was a ditch. If he could get across the ditch he could easily scramble among the slanted pines, climb from one to the next, get past the log jam and hop the ditch back to the road.

One look at the ditch finished that. Barton closed his eyes and hung on tight.

The ditch wasn't wide; he *might* be able to vault it. But there was no bottom. He was standing over a bottomless gulf. He stepped back, away from it, and stood breathing quickly and clutching his cigarette. It went down forever. Like looking up at the sky. No limit. A ceaseless drop that finally blurred into a dim, ominous chaos.

He forgot about the ditch and turned his attention back to the logs. A car didn't stand a chance of getting past, but maybe a man on foot could negotiate his way to the other side. If he could get half way he could halt at the truck, sit in the cabin and rest. Divide it into two separate jobs.

He approached the logs gingerly. The first wasn't so bad, small and fairly steady. He stepped onto it, caught hold with his hands, and jumped to the next. Under him, the mass shuddered ominously. Barton quickly scrambled to the next and clung tight. So far so good. The one ahead was a big baby, old and dry and cracked. It jutted up at a steep angle, piled on three beneath it. Like spilled matches.

He jumped. The log split, and he frantically leaped off again. Desperately, he clutched for purchase. His fingers slipped; he fell back. He dug in wildly, trying to draw his body up on a flat surface.

He made it.

Gasping, panting for breath, Barton lay stretched out on the log, waves of relief flooding over him. Finally, he pulled himself to a sitting position. If he could go a little farther he should be able to catch hold of the truck itself. Pull himself onto it. That would be half way. He could rest . . .

He was as far away as before. No closer. For a moment he doubted his sanity; then understanding came. He had got turned around. The logs were a maze. He had got off in the wrong direction, ceased moving toward the truck. He had moved in a closed circle.

The hell with getting out. All he wanted now was to get back to his car. Get back where he had started from. Logs were on all sides of him. Piles and heaps and jutting snouts. Good God, he hadn't come that far in, had he? Was it possible he had got himself in so deep? He was yards from the edge; surely he hadn't managed to crawl that far.

He began crawling around, back the way he had come.

The logs swayed and tilted dangerously under him. Fear made him nervous. He lost his grip and fell between two of them. For a blinding, terrifying instant he was underneath, the sunlight was cut off and he was in a closing cave of darkness. He pushed up with all his strength, and one of the logs gave. He scrambled wildly back up, emerged into the sunlight, and lay outstretched, gasping and shuddering.

He lay for an indefinite period. He had lost track of time. The next thing he knew, a voice was speaking to him.

'Mr Barton! Mr Barton! Can you hear me?'

He managed to raise his head. Standing on the road, beyond the logs, was Peter Trilling. He grinned calmly at Barton, hands on his hips, face gleaming and tanned in the bright sunlight. He didn't seem especially worried. In fact, he looked rather pleased.

'Help me,' Barton gasped.

'What are you doing out there?'

'I tried to get across.' Barton pulled himself up to a sitting position. 'How the hell am I going to get back?'

And then he noticed something. It wasn't the middle of the day. It was early evening. The sun was setting over the far hills, the giant figure that loomed up at the opposite end of the valley. He examined his wristwatch. It was six-thirty. He had been on the logs seven hours.

'You shouldn't have tried to get across,' Peter said, as he cautiously approached. 'If they don't want you to get out you shouldn't try.'

'I got *in* this damn valley!'

'They must have wanted you in. But they don't want you out. You better be careful. You might get stuck in there and die of starvation.' Peter obviously enjoyed the spectacle. But after a moment he leaped agilely up on the first log and picked his way over to Barton.

Barton got unsteadily to his feet. He was scared clean

through. This was his first taste of the powers that operated in the valley. Gratefully, he took hold of Peter's small hand and allowed the boy to lead him back to the edge.

Oddly, it took only a few seconds.

'Thank God.' He wiped his forehead and picked up his coat, where he had tossed it. The air was turning chill; it was cold and late. 'I won't try that again, for a while.'

'You better not try it again *ever*,' Peter said quietly.

Something in the boy's voice made Barton's head jerk up. 'What do you mean?'

'Just what I say. You were there seven hours.' Peter's confident smile broadened. 'I was the one who kept you there. I twisted you up in time.'

Barton absorbed the information slowly. 'It was you? But you finally got me out.'

'Sure,' Peter said easily. 'I kept you in and I got you out. When it pleased me. I wanted you to see who was boss.'

There was a long silence. The boy's confident smile grew. He was pleased with himself. He had really done a good job.

'I saw you from my ledge,' he explained. 'I knew where you were going. I figured you'd try to walk across.' His chest swelled. 'Nobody can do that except me. I'm the only one.' A cunning film slid over his eyes. 'I have ways.'

'Drop dead,' Barton said. He strode past the boy and hopped in the Packard. As he gunned the motor and released the brake he saw the confident smile falter. By the time he had the car turned around toward Millgate it had become a nervous grimace.

'Aren't you going to ride me back?' Peter demanded, hurrying up to the window. His face turned sickly white.

56

'A lot of those death's-head moths down at the foot of the hill. It's almost night!'

'Too bad,' Barton said, and shot the car down the road.

Lethal hatred flashed over Peter's face. He was lost behind, a dwindling column of violent animosity.

Barton was sweating hard. Maybe he had made a mistake. It had been plenty uncomfortable out there in the maze of logs, crawling around and around like a bug in a water glass. The kid had a lot of power and he was mad enough to start using it. On top of that there were all his other troubles; he was stuck here, whether he liked it or not.

For the next day or so, it was going to be close quarters.

Millgate was dissolving into gloomy darkness as Barton turned onto Jefferson Street. Most of the shops were closed. Drugstores, hardware stores, grocery stores, endless cafes and cheap bars.

He parked in front of the Magnolia Club, a run-down joint that looked ready to collapse any minute. A few bucolic toughs lounged around the front. Stubble-chinned and shiftless, their eyes glittered at him, red and penetrating, as he locked the Packard and pushed the swinging doors of the bar aside.

Only a couple of men were at the bar. The tables were empty; the chairs were still piled up on them, legs sticking forlornly up. He seated himself at the back end of the bar, where nobody would bother him, and ordered three quick bourbons, one after another.

He was in a hell of a mess. He had come in, and now he couldn't get out. He was stuck fast. Caught inside the valley by the spilled load of lumber. How long had it been there? Good God, it might stay there forever. Not to mention his cosmic enemy, the one who had manipulated his memories, and Peter, his earthly enemy thrown in for extra humor.

The bourbons made him calmer. They – it, the cosmic power – wanted him for some reason. Maybe he was *supposed* to find out who he was. Maybe it had all been planned, his coming here, returning to Millgate after so many years. Maybe his every move, everything he had ever done, his whole life . . .

He ordered a new batch of bourbons; he had plenty to forget. More men had filed in. Hunched-over men in leather jackets. Brooding over their beer. Not talking or moving. Prepared to spend the evening. Barton ignored them and concentrated on his purposeful drinking.

He was just starting to toss down the sixth bourbon when he realized one of the men was watching him. Numbly, he pretended not to notice. Good God, didn't he have enough troubles?

The man had turned around on his stool. A grimy-faced old drunk. Tall and stooped. In a torn, seedy-looking coat, filthy trousers. The remains of shoes. His hands were large and dark, fingers creased with countless cuts. His befuddled eyes were fixed intently on Barton, watching every move he made. He didn't look away, even when Barton glared hostilely back.

The man got up and came unsteadily over. Barton braced himself. He was going to get touched for a drink. The man sat down on the next stool with a sigh and folded his hands. 'Hi,' he grunted, blowing a cloud of alcoholic breath around Barton. He pushed his damp, pale hair back out of his eyes. Thin hair, as moist and limp as corn silk. His eyes were cloudy blue, like a child's. 'How are you?'

'What do you want?' Barton demanded bluntly, driven to the edge of drunken despair.

'Scotch and water will do.'

Barton was taken aback. 'Look here, buddy,' he began, but the man cut him off with his mild, gentle voice.

'I guess you don't remember me.'

Barton blinked. 'Remember you?'

'You were running down the street. Yesterday. You were looking for Central.'

Barton placed him. The drunk who had laughed. 'Oh, yeah,' he said slowly.

The man beamed. 'See? You do remember me.' He put out his grimy, seamed paw. 'My name's Christopher. William Christopher.' He added, 'I'm a poor old Swede.'

Barton declined the hand. 'I can do without your company.'

Christopher grinned thickly. 'I believe you. But maybe if I get the Scotch and water the exhilaration will be too much for me and I'll have to leave.'

Barton waved over the bartender. 'Scotch and water,' he muttered. 'For him.'

'Did you ever find Central?' Christopher asked.

'No.'

Christopher giggled in a shrill, high-pitched voice. 'I'm not surprised. I could have told you that.'

'You did.'

The drink came, and Christopher accepted it gratefully. 'Good stuff,' he observed, taking a big swallow and then a gulp of air. 'You're from out of town, aren't you?'

'You guessed it.'

'Why did you come to Millgate? A little town like this. Nobody ever comes here.'

Barton raised his head moodily. 'I came here to find myself.'

For some reason, that struck Christopher as funny. He shrieked, loud and shrill, until the others at the bar turned in annoyance.

'What's eating you?' Barton demanded angrily. 'What the hell's so funny about that?'

Christopher managed to calm himself. 'Find yourself? You have any clues? Will you know yourself when you find yourself? What do you look like?' He burst into laughter again, in spite of his efforts. Barton sank down farther, and hunched miserably around his glass.

'Cut it out,' he muttered. 'I have enough trouble already.'

'Trouble? What sort of trouble?'

'Everything. Every goddamn thing in the world.' The bourbons were really beginning to work their enchantment on him. 'Christ, I might as well be dead. First I find out I'm dead, that I never lived to grow up – '

Christopher shook his head. 'That's bad.'

'Then those two goddamn luminous people come walking through the porch.'

'Wanderers. Yeah, they give you a start, the first time. But you get used to them.'

'Then that damn kid goes around looking for bees. And he shows me a guy fifty miles high. With his head made out of an electric light bulb.'

A change came over Christopher. Through his wheezy drunkenness something gleamed. An intent core of awareness. 'Oh?' he said. 'What guy is that?'

'Biggest goddamn guy you ever saw.' Barton made a wild sweep. 'A million miles high. Knock the living daylights out of you. Made out of daylight, himself.'

Christopher sipped his drink slowly. 'What else happened to you, Mr – '

'Barton. Ted Barton. Then I fell off a log.'

'You *what*?'

'I went log rolling.' Barton slumped forward wretchedly. 'I got lost in a puddle of logs seven hours. A little creep led me out again.' He wiped his eyes miserably with the back of his hand. 'And I never found Central Street. Or Pine Street.' His voice rose with wild despair. 'Goddammit, I was *born* on Pine Street! There must be such a place!'

For a moment Christopher said nothing. He finished his drink, turned the glass upside down on the counter, spun it thoughtfully, then pushed it abruptly aside. 'No, you won't find Pine Street,' he said. 'Or Central. At least, not anymore.'

The words penetrated. Barton sat up, his brain suddenly ice cold, even through his alcoholic mist. 'What do you mean, *not anymore*?'

'It's been gone a long time. Years and years.' The old man rubbed his wrinkled forehead wearily. 'I haven't heard that street talked about for a long time.' His baby-blue eyes were fixed intently on Barton; he was trying to concentrate through the haze of whisky and time. 'Funny, to hear that old name again. I had almost forgotten. You know, Barton, there must be something wrong.'

'Yes,' Barton agreed tensely. 'There's something wrong. *What is it?*'

Christopher rubbed his lined forehead, trying to bring his thoughts together. 'I don't know. Something big.' He glanced around fearfully. 'Maybe I'm out of my mind. Pine Street was a nice place. A lot nicer than Fairmount. That's what they have there now. Fairmount. Not the same houses at all. Not the same street. And nobody remembers.' Tears filled his blue eyes and he wiped them miserably away. 'Nobody remembers except you and me. Nobody in the whole world. *What the hell are we going to do?*'

61

# SEVEN

Barton was breathing quickly. 'Listen to me. Stop whimpering and listen!'

Christopher shuddered. 'Yes. Sorry, Barton. This whole thing has – '

Barton grabbed him by the arm. 'Then it really *was* the way I remember. Pine Street. Central. The old park. My memories aren't false!'

Christopher mopped his eyes with a filthy handkerchief. 'Yes, the old park. You remember that? Good God, what's happened around here?' All the color had drained from his face, leaving it a sickly yellow. 'What's wrong with them? Why don't they remember?' Terror shuddered through him. 'And they're not the same people. The old ones are gone. Like the places. All but you and me.'

'I left,' Barton said. 'When I was nine.' Abruptly he got to his feet. 'Let's get out of here. Where can we talk?'

Christopher assembled himself. 'My place. We can talk there.' He jumped off the stool and moved quickly toward the door. Barton followed close behind.

The street was cool and dark. Occasional streetlights spluttered at irregular intervals. A few people were strolling along, mostly men between bars.

Christopher hurried down a side street. Barton had trouble keeping up with him. 'I've waited eighteen years for this,' Christopher gasped. 'I thought I was crazy. I didn't tell anybody. I was afraid. All these years – and it was true.'

'When did the Change come?'

'Eighteen years ago.'

'Slowly?'

'Suddenly. Overnight. I woke up and it was all different. I couldn't find my way around. I stayed inside and hid. I thought I was crazy.'

'Nobody else remembered?'

'Everyone was gone!'

Barton was stunned. 'You mean – '

'How could they remember? They were gone, too. Everything was changed, even the people. A whole new town.'

'Did you know about the barrier?'

'I knew nobody could get out or in. There's something across the road. But they don't care. There's something wrong with them.'

'Who are the Wanderers?' Barton demanded.

'I don't know.'

'When did they appear? Before the Change?'

'No. After the Change. I never saw them before that. Everyone seems to think they're perfectly natural.'

'Who are the two giants?'

Christopher shook his head. 'I don't know. Once I thought I saw something. I had gone up the road, looking for a way out. I had to stop; there was a stalled lumber truck.'

'That's the barrier.'

Christopher swore. 'Good God! That was years ago! And it's still there . . .'

They had gone several blocks. Darkness was all around them. Vague shapes of houses. Occasional lights. The houses were run-down and shabby. Barton noticed with increasing surprise how rickety they were; he didn't remember this part of town as being so bad.

'Everything is worse!' he said.

'That's right. This wasn't nearly so bad before the Change. It looked pretty good, in fact. My place was a nice little three-room cabin; I built it myself. Wired it, put in plumbing, fixed the roof up fine. That morning I woke up and what was I living in?' The old man halted and fumbled for his key. 'A packing crate. Wasn't nothing more than a packing crate. Not even a foundation. I remember pouring that foundation. Took me a whole week to get it right. And now nothing but a mud sill.'

He found the key and in the darkness located the handle of the door. He fooled around, muttering and cursing. Finally the door squeaked back, and he and Barton entered.

Christopher lit an oil lamp. 'No electricity. What do you think of that? After all my work. I tell you, Barton, this thing's diabolical. All the hard work I did. All the things I had, everything I built up. Wiped out overnight. Now I'm nothing. I didn't drink before. Get that? Not a drop.'

The place was a shack, nothing more. A single room; stove and sink at one end, bed at the other. Junk was littered everywhere. Dirty dishes, packages and boxes of food, bags of eggshells and garbage, moldy bread, newspapers, magazines, dirty clothes, empty bottles, endless old furniture crowded together. And wiring.

'Yeah,' Christopher said. 'I've been trying for eighteen years to wire the goddamn place again.' There was fear on his face, naked, hopeless fear. 'I used to be a hell of a good electrician. Serviced radios. Ran a little radio shop.'

'Sure,' Barton said. 'Will's Sales and Service.'

'Gone. Completely gone. There's a hand laundry there now. On Jefferson Street, as it's called now. Do a terrible job. Ruin your shirts. Nothing left of my radio shop. I woke up that morning, started off to work.

Thought something was odd. Got there and found a goddamn laundry. Steam irons and pants pressers.'

Barton picked up a portable B battery. Pliers, solder, a soldering iron, paste, spaghetti, a signal generator, radio tubes, bottles of condensers, resistors, schematics – everything. 'And you can't get this place wired?'

'I try.' Christopher examined his hands miserably. 'It's gone. I fumble around. Break things. Drop things. Forget what I'm doing. Mislay my wire. Step on and break my tools.'

'Why?'

Christopher's eyes glittered with terror. 'They don't want me to bring it back. To make it like it was. I was supposed to be changed like the others. I *was* changed, partly. I wasn't all run-down, like this. I was hardworking. Had my shop and my ability. Led a good clean life. Barton, they stop me from fixing it up. They practically take the soldering iron out of my hands.'

Barton pushed aside a litter of cables and insulation and sat down on the edge of the work bench. 'They got part of you. Then they have some power over you.'

Christopher rummaged excitedly in a cluttered cupboard. 'This thing hangs over Millgate like a black fog! A filthy black fog, creeping in all the windows and doors. It's destroyed this town. These people are imitation people. The real ones are gone. Swept aside overnight.' He got out a dusty wine bottle and waved it in front of Barton. 'By God, I'm going to celebrate! Join in, Barton. I've been keeping this bottle for years.'

Barton examined the wine bottle. He blew dust from its label and held it up to the oil lamp. It was old, plenty old. Imported muscatel. 'I don't know,' he said doubtfully. He was already beginning to feel sick from the bourbons. 'I don't like to mix my drinks.'

'This is a celebration.' Christopher spilled a heap of rubbish onto the floor and found a corkscrew. The bottle between his knees, he expertly speared the cork and began twisting it out. 'Celebration for you and me finding each other.'

The wine wasn't too good. Barton sipped a little from his glass and studied the aged, seamed face of the old man. Christopher was slumped over in his chair, brooding. He drank rapidly, automatically, from his not quite clean glass.

'No,' he said. 'They don't want all this changed back. They did this to us. Took away our town. Our friends.' His face hardened. 'The bastards won't let us lift a finger to fix things up again. They think they're so damn big.'

'But I got in here,' Barton murmured. He was getting pretty dopy; the bourbons and wine, mixed up together. 'Got past the barrier, somehow.'

'They're not perfect.' Christopher lurched to his feet and put down his glass. 'Missed most of me and let you in. Asleep at the switch, like anybody else.'

He pulled open the bottom drawer of a dresser and tossed out clothing and parcels. At the bottom was a sealed box. An old silverware chest. Grunting and perspiring, Christopher lugged it out and dumped it on the table.

'I'm not hungry,' Barton muttered. 'Just like to sit here and – '

'Watch.' Christopher got a tiny key from his wallet; with extreme care he fitted it in the microscopic lock and pushed the lid up. 'I'm going to show it to you, Barton. You're my only friend. Only person in the world I can trust.'

It wasn't silverware. The thing was intricate. Wires and struts, complicated meters and switches. A cone of metal, carefully soldered together. Christopher lifted it out and pushed braces into their catches. He ran the cables over to the B battery and screwed the terminal caps into place.

'The shades,' he grunted. 'Pull them down. Don't want *them* to see this.' He tittered nervously. 'They'd give a lot to get hold of this. Think they're smart, got everybody under their thumb. Not quite everybody.'

He threw a switch and the cone hummed ominously. The hum turned to a whine as he fooled with the controls. Barton edged away uneasily. 'What the hell is it, a bomb? You going to blow them all up?'

A crafty look slid over the old man's face. 'I'll tell you later. Have to be careful.' He ran around the room, pulling down the shades, peering out; he locked the door and came carefully back to his humming cone. Barton was down on his hands and knees, peering into its works. It was a maze of intricate wiring, a regular web of glowing metal. Across the front was lettered:

S. R.
Do Not Touch
Property of Will Christopher

Christopher assumed a solemn manner. He squatted down beside Barton, his legs tucked under him. Gingerly, almost reverently, he lifted the cone, held it in his hands a moment, and then fitted it over his head. He gazed out from under it, blue eyes unblinking, weathered face serious with the importance of the occasion. His expression sagged a little, as the hum of the cone dropped into silence.

'Damn.' He struggled up and groped for his soldering iron. 'Loose connection.'

Barton leaned against the wall and waited sleepily, while Christopher resoldered the connection. Presently the hum sounded again, a little ragged, but quite loud. Louder than before.

'Barton,' Christopher grated. 'You're ready?'

'Sure,' Barton muttered. He opened one eye and focused on the happenings.

Christopher got down the old wine bottle from the table. He placed it carefully on the floor and seated himself beside it, the cone on his head. It came down to his eyebrows, and it was heavy. He adjusted it a little, then folded his arms and concentrated on the wine bottle.

'What's – ' Barton began, but the old man cut him angrily off.

'Don't talk. Have to summon all my faculties.' His eyes half closed. His jaw locked. His brow wrinkled. He took a deep breath and held it.

Silence.

Barton found himself gradually fading off into sleep. He tried to watch the wine bottle, but its slender, dusty shape wavered and dimmed. He stifled a yawn and then belched. Christopher shot him a furious look and quickly returned to his concentrating. Barton mumbled an apology. He really yawned, then. Loud and long. The room, the old man, and especially the wine bottle, receded and blurred. The humming lulled him. Like a swarm of bees. Constant and penetrating.

He could hardly see the bottle. It was only a vague shape. He summoned his attention, but it rapidly leaked away. Damn it, he couldn't see the bottle now at all. He struggled up and forced his eyes open. It didn't help. The bottle was a mere blur, just the trace of a shadow on the floor in front of Christopher.

'Sorry,' Barton muttered. 'Can't make out the damn thing anymore.'

Christopher didn't answer. His face was dark lavender;

he looked ready to explode. His whole being was concentrated on the spot the wine bottle had occupied. Straining and glowering, knitting his brows, breathing hoarsely between his teeth, fists clenched, body rigid . . .

It was beginning to come back. Barton felt better. There it was, wavering back into view. The shadow became a blur. Then a dark cube. The cube solidified, gained color and form, became opaque; he couldn't see the floor beyond anymore. Barton sighed with relief. Good to see the damn thing again. He settled back against the wall and made himself comfortable.

There was only one problem. It needled at him, made him vaguely uncomfortable. The thing forming on the floor in front of Christopher wasn't the dusty bottle of muscatel. It was something else.

An incredibly ancient coffee-grinder.

Christopher pulled the cone from his head. He sighed, a long drawn-out whistle of triumph. 'I did it, Barton,' he said. 'There it is.'

Barton shook his head. 'I don't understand.' A cold chill was beginning to pluck at him. 'Where's the bottle? What happened to the wine bottle?'

'There never was a wine bottle,' Christopher said.

'But I – '

'Fake. Distortion.' Christopher spat with disgust. 'That's my old coffee-grinder. My grandmother brought that over from Sweden. I told you I didn't drink before the Change.'

Understanding came to Barton. 'This coffee-grinder turned into a wine bottle when the Change came. But – '

'But underneath it was still a coffee-grinder.' Christopher got unsteadily to his feet; he looked exhausted. 'You see, Barton?'

Barton saw. 'The old town's still here.'

'Yes. It wasn't destroyed. It was buried. It's under the surface. There's a layer over it. A dark fog. Illusion. They came and laid this black cloud over everything. But the real town's underneath. *And it can be brought back.*'

'S. R. Spell Remover.'

'That's right.' Christopher patted the cone proudly. 'That's my Spell Remover. Built it myself. Nobody knows about it except me and you.'

Barton reached out and picked up the coffee-grinder. It was firm and hard. Ancient, scarred wood. Metal wheel. It smelled of coffee. A pungent, musty odor that tickled his nostrils. He turned the wheel a little, and the mechanism whirred. A few grains of coffee fell from it.

'So it's still here,' he said softly.

'Yes. It's still here.'

'How did you find out?'

Christopher got out his pipe and filled it slowly, hands shaking with fatigue. 'I was pretty discouraged at first. Finding everything changed, everybody different. Didn't know nobody. Couldn't talk to them; didn't understand me. Started going down to the Magnolia Club every night; nothing else to do, without my radio shop. Came home pretty blind one night. Sat down, right where I'm sitting now. Started remembering the old days. Old places and people. How my little house used to be. While I was thinking about it, this shack began to fade out. And my sweet little house faded in.'

He lit his pipe and sucked at it solemnly.

'I ran around like a crazy thing. I was happy as hell. But it began to leave. Faded back out again, and this damn hovel reappeared.' He kicked at a littered table. 'Like you see it. Filthy junk. When I think of how it was . . .'

'You remember Berg's Jewelry Store?'·

70

'Sure. On Central Street. It's gone, of course. There's a cheap run-down hash-house in its place. A joint.'

Barton got the bit of stale bread from his pocket. 'That explains it. Why my compass turned into *this* when I entered the valley. It came from Berg's Jewelry Store.' He tossed the bread away. 'And the Spell Remover?'

'Took me fifteen years to build it. They made my hands so damn clumsy. Could hardly solder stuff. Had to repeat the same process again and again. It focuses my mind. My memories. So I can direct my thoughts. Like a lens. That way, I can bring a thing all the way up. Bring it up from the depths. To the surface. The fog lifts and it's there again, like it was before. Like it ought to be.'

Barton got down his wine glass. It had been half full, but now there was nothing in it. The untasted wine had vanished with the bottle. He sniffed it. The glass smelled faintly of coffee.

'You've done pretty well,' Barton said.

'I guess so. It was hard. I'm not completely free. They hold part of me. Wish I had a picture of this place to show you. The tile sink I put in. That was really a dream.'

Barton turned the empty glass over and shook out a grain of coffee. 'You're going on, of course.'

'Oh?'

'With this; what can stop you? Good God, man, you can bring it all back.'

Christopher's face sagged. 'Barton, I've got something to tell you.'

But he didn't have to. Abruptly, warm wine spilled down Barton's sleeve and over his fingers and wrist. At the same time the coffee-grinder faded out, and the muscatel bottle reappeared. Dusty and slim and half-full of wine.

71

'It doesn't last,' Christopher said sadly. 'Not more than ten minutes. I can't keep it going.'

Barton washed his hands at the sink. 'It always does that?'

'Always. Never completely hardens. Can't quite lock the real thing into place. I guess I'm just not strong enough. They're pretty big, whoever they are.'

Barton dried his hands on a filthy towel. He was deep in thought. 'Maybe it's just this one object. Have you tried the Spell Remover on anything else?'

Christopher scrambled up and crossed over to the dresser. He rummaged around in the drawer and got out a small cardboard box. He carried it back and sat down on the floor with it.

'Look at this.' He opened the box and lifted out something. With trembling fingers he removed the tissue paper. Barton crouched down and peered over his shoulder.

In the tissue paper was a ball of brown string. Knotted and frazzled. Wound around a bit of wood.

His old face awed, eyes glittering, lips half-parted, Christopher ran his fingers over the ball of string. 'I've tried on this. Many times. Every week or so I try. I'd give anything if I could bring this back. But I can't get so much as a flicker.'

Barton took the string from the old man's hand. 'What the hell is it? Looks like ordinary string.'

A significant look settled over Christopher's tired face. 'Barton, that was Aaron Northrup's tire iron.'

Barton raised his eyes unbelievingly. 'Good Lord.'

'Yes. It's true. I stole it. Nobody else knew what it was. I had to search for it. Remember, the tire iron was over the door of the Millgate Merchants' Bank.'

'Yes. The mayor put it up there. I remember that day. I was just a little kid then.'

72

'That was a long time ago. The Bank's gone now, of course. There's a ladies' tea room in its place. And this ball of string over the door. I stole it one night. Didn't mean a thing to anyone else.' Christopher turned away, overcome by his emotions. 'Nobody else remembers Aaron Northrup's tire iron.'

Barton's own eyes were moist. 'I was only seven years old when it happened.'

'Did you see it?'

'I saw it. Bob O'Neill yelled down Central at the top of his lungs. I was in the candy shop.'

Christopher nodded eagerly. 'I was fixing an old At-water Kent. I heard the bastard. Yelled like a stuck pig. Audible for miles.'

Barton's face glowed. 'Then I saw the crook run past. His car wouldn't start.'

'No, he was too damn nervous. O'Neill yelled, and the crook just ran straight down the middle of the street.'

'With the money in that paper sack, in his arms. Like a sack of groceries.'

'He was from Chicago. One of those racketeers.'

'A Sicilian. A big-time gangster. I saw him run past the candy store. I ran outside. Bob O'Neill was standing there in front of the Bank, shouting his head off.'

'Everybody was running and hollering. Like a bunch of donkeys.'

Barton's vision grew dim. 'The crook ran down Fulton Street. And there was old Northrup, changing the tire on his model T Ford.'

'Yeah, he was in from his farm again. To get loaded up with cattle feed. He was sitting there on the curb with his jack and tire iron.' Christopher took the ball of string back and held it gently in his hand. 'The crook tried to run past him – '

'And old Northrup leaped up and hit him over the head.'

'He was a tall old man.'

'Over six feet. Thin, though. Rangy old farmer. He really cracked that crook a mean one.'

'He had a good wrist. From cranking his old Ford. I guess it just about killed the fellow.'

'Multiple concussion. A tire iron's pretty heavy.' Barton took back the ball of string and touched it gently. 'So this is it. Aaron Northrup's tire iron. The Bank paid him five hundred dollars for it. And Mayor Clayton nailed it up over the door of the Bank. There was that big ceremony.'

'Everybody was there.'

Barton's chest swelled. 'I held the ladder.' He trembled. 'Christopher, I had hold of that tire iron. As Jack Wakeley was climbing up with the hammer and nails, they gave it to me and I passed it on up. I touched it.'

'You're touching it now,' Christopher said with feeling. 'That's it.'

For a long time Barton gazed down at the ball of string. 'I remember it. I held it. It was heavy.'

'Yeah, it weighed a lot.'

Barton got to his feet. He laid the ball of string carefully on the table. He removed his coat and put it over the back of a chair.

'What are you going to do?' Christopher demanded anxiously.

There was a strange look on Barton's face. Resolve, mixed with dreamy recollection. 'I'll tell you,' he said. 'I'm going to remove the spell. I'm going to bring back the tire iron, the way it was.'

# EIGHT

Christopher turned down the oil lamp until the room was almost dark. He set the lamp next to the ball of string and then moved back, into the corner.

Barton stood close to the table, eyes on the string. He had never tried to lift a spell before; it was a new experience for him. But he remembered the tire iron. He remembered how it had felt, how it had looked. The sights and sounds of the robbery itself. Old man Northrup leaping up and swinging it over his head. The iron coming down. The Sicilian stretched out on the pavement. The ceremony. Everybody cheering. The iron briefly in his hands.

He concentrated. He summoned all his memories together and focused them on the limp ball of brown string, knotted and frayed, on the table beside the lamp. He imagined the iron there instead of the string. Long and black and metallic. And heavy. Solid metal.

No one moved. Christopher wasn't even breathing. Barton held his body rigid; he put everything into it. All his mental strength. He thought of the old town, the real town. It wasn't gone. It was still there; it was *here*, around him, under him, on all sides. Beneath the blanket of illusion. The layer of black fog. The town still lived.

Within the ball of string was Aaron Northrup's tire iron.

Time passed. The room became cold. Someplace far off, a clock struck. Christopher's pipe faded and dimmed into cold ash. Barton shivered a little and went on. He thought of every aspect of it. Every sensation, visual, tactile, audible . . .

Christopher gasped. 'It wavered.'

The ball of string had hesitated. A certain insubstantiality crept over it. Barton strained with all his might. Everything flickered – the whole room, the gloomy shadows beyond the lamp.

'*Again,*' Christopher gasped. 'Keep on. Don't stop.'

He didn't stop. And presently, silently, the ball of string faded. The wall became visible behind it; he could see the table beneath. For a moment there was nothing but a misty shadow. A vague presence, left behind.

'I never got this far,' Christopher whispered, in awe. 'Couldn't do it.'

Barton didn't answer. He kept his attention on the spot. The tire iron. It had to come. He drew it out, demanded it come forth. It had to come. It was there, underneath the illusion.

A long shadow flickered. Longer than the string. A foot and a half long. It wavered, then became more distinct.

'There it is!' Christopher gasped. 'It's coming!'

It was coming, all right. Barton concentrated until black spots danced in front of his eyes. The tire iron was on its way. It turned black, opaque. Glittered a little in the light of the oil lamp. And then . . .

With a furious clang the tire iron crashed to the floor and lay.

Christopher ran forward and scooped it up. He was trembling and wiping his eyes. 'Barton, you did it. You made it come back.'

Barton sagged. 'Yes. That's it. Exactly the way I remember it.'

Christopher ran his hands up and down the metal bar. 'Aaron Northrup's old tire iron. I haven't seen it in

76

eighteen years. Not since that day. I couldn't make it come back, Barton. But you did it.'

'I remembered it,' Barton grunted. He wiped his forehead shakily; he was perspiring and weak. 'Maybe better than you. I actually held it. And my memory always was good.'

'And you weren't here.'

'No. I wasn't touched by the Change. I'm not distorted at all.'

Christopher's old face glowed. 'Now we can go on, Barton. There's nothing to stop us. The whole town. We can bring it back, piece by piece. Everthing we remember.'

'I don't know it all,' Barton muttered. 'A few places I never saw.'

'Maybe I remember them. Between us we probably remember the whole town.'

'Maybe we can find somebody else. Get a complete map of the old town. Reconstruct it.'

Christopher put down the tire iron. 'I'll build a Spell Remover for both of us. One for each of us. I'll build hundreds of them, all sizes and shapes. With both of us wearing them . . .' His voice faded and died. A sick look settled slowly over his face.

'What's the matter?' Barton demanded, suddenly apprehensive. 'What's wrong?'

'The Spell Remover.' Christopher sat numbly down at the table. He picked up the Spell Remover. 'You didn't have it on.'

Christopher turned up the lamp. 'It wasn't the Spell Remover,' he managed to say finally. He looked old and broken; he moved feebly. 'All these years. It wasn't any good.'

'No,' Barton said. 'I guess it wasn't.'

'But *why?*' Christopher appealed helplessly. 'How did you do it?'

Barton didn't hear him. His mind was racing wildly. Abruptly he got to his feet. 'We've got to find out,' he said.

'Yes,' Christopher agreed, pulling himself together with a violent effort. He fooled aimlessly with the tire iron, then suddenly held it out to Barton. 'Here.'

'What?'

'It's yours, Barton. Not mine. It never really belonged to me.'

After a moment Barton slowly accepted it. 'All right. I'll take it. I know what has to be done. There's a hell of a lot ahead of us.' He began to pace restlessly back and forth, the tire iron gripped like a battle axe. 'We've been sitting around here long enough. We've got to get moving.'

'Moving?'

'We've got to make sure we can do it. In a big way.' Barton impatiently waved the tire iron. 'One object. My God, this is only the beginning. We've got a whole town to reconstruct!'

Christopher nodded slowly. 'Yes. That's a lot.'

'Maybe we can't do it.' Barton pulled the door open; cold night wind billowed in. 'Come on.'

'Where are we going?'

Barton was already outside. 'We're going to make a real attempt. Something big. Something important.'

Christopher hurried after him. 'You're right. The Spell Remover doesn't matter. It's *doing* it that's important. If you can do it your way . . .'

'What'll we try?' Barton pushed his way impatiently along the dark street, still holding tightly onto the tire iron. 'We have to know what it was before the Change.'

'I've had time to figure most of this neighborhood out. I've been able to map this part of town. That over there,' Christopher indicated a tall house, 'that was a garage and auto repair place. And down there, all those old deserted stores – '

'What were they?' Barton increased his pace. 'My God, they look awful. What was there? What's underneath them?'

'Don't you remember?' Christopher said softly.

It took a moment. Barton had to look up at the dark hills to get his bearings. 'I'm not certain . . .' he began. And then it came.

Eighteen years was a long time. But he had never forgotten the old park with its cannon. He had played there many times. Eaten lunch there with his mother and father. Hidden in the thick grass, played cowboys and Indians with the other kids of the town.

In the faint light, he could make out a row of drooping, decayed old shacks. Ancient stores, no longer used. Missing boards. Windows broken. A few tattered rags fluttering in the night wind. Shabby, rotting shapes in which birds nested, rats and mice scampered.

'They look old,' Christopher said softly. 'Fifty or sixty years old. But they weren't here before the Change. That was the park.'

Barton crossed the street toward it. 'It began over this way. At this corner. What's it called, now?'

'Dudley Street is the new name.' Christopher was excited. 'The cannon was in the center. There was a stack of cannon balls! It was an old cannon from the War Between the States. Lee dragged that cannon around Richmond.'

The two of them stood close together, remembering how it had been. The park and the cannon. The old town, the real town that had existed. For a while neither of them spoke. Each was wrapped up in his own thoughts.

Then Barton moved away. 'I'll go down to this end. It started at Milton and Jones.'

'Now it's Dudley and Rutledge.' Christopher shook himself into activity. 'I'll take this end.'

Barton reached the corner and halted. In the gloom he could barely make out the figure of Will Christopher. The old man was waving. 'Tell me when to begin!' Christopher shouted.

'Begin now.' Impatience filled Barton. Enough time had been wasted – eighteen years. 'Concentrate on that end. I'll work on this end.'

'You think we can do it? A public park is an awful big thing.'

'Damn big,' Barton said under his breath. He faced the ancient, ruined stores and summoned all his strength. At the other end, Will Christopher did the same.

# NINE

Mary was curled up on her bed, reading a magazine, when the Wanderer appeared.

It came from the wall and slowly crossed the room, eyes shut tight, fists clenched, lips moving. Mary put down her magazine at once and got quickly to her feet. This was a Wanderer she had never seen before. An older woman, perhaps forty. Tall and heavy, with gray hair and thick breasts under her rough one-piece garment. Her stern face was twisted in a deadly serious expression; her lips continued to move as she crossed the room, passed through the big chair, and then disappeared through the far wall without a sound.

Mary's heart thudded. The Wanderer was looking for her, but she had gone too far. It was hard to tell exactly; and she couldn't open her eyes. She was counting, trying to get the place exactly right.

Mary hurried out of the room, down the hall and outside. She ran around the side of the house, to the place opposite her own room. As she waited for the Wanderer to emerge she couldn't help thinking of the one who had gone too far, but not far enough to be outside the house. He had opened his eyes within the wall, apparently. In any case, he had never emerged. And there had been a loathsome smell for weeks after.

Something gleamed. It was a dark night; a few faint stars shone down. The Wanderer was coming out, all right. Moving slowly and cautiously. Getting ready to open her eyes. She was tense. Nervous. Her muscles strained. Lips twitched. Abruptly her eyelids fluttered – and she was gazing around her in wild relief.

'Here I am,' Mary said quickly, hurrying up to her.

The Wanderer sank down on a stone. 'Thank God. I was afraid . . .' She looked nervously around. 'I did go too far, didn't I? We're outside.'

'It's all right. What did you want?'

The Wanderer began to relax a little. 'It's a nice night. But cold. Shouldn't you have a sweater on?' After a moment she added, 'I'm Hilda. You've never seen me before.'

'No,' Mary agreed. 'But I know who you are.' She sat down close to the Wanderer. Now that she had opened her eyes, Hilda looked like anyone else. She had lost her faintly luminous quality; she was substantial. Mary reached out her hand and touched the Wanderer's arm. Firm and solid. And warm. She smiled, and the Wanderer smiled back at her.

'How old are you, Mary?' she asked.

'Thirteen.'

The Wanderer rumpled the girl's thick black curls. 'You're a lovely child. I would think you had plenty of fellows. Although maybe you're too young for that.'

'You wanted to see me, didn't you?' Mary asked politely. She was a little impatient; somebody might come, and in addition, she was sure something important was happening. 'What was it about?'

'We need information.'

Mary repressed a sigh. 'What sort of information?'

'As you know, we've made progress. Everything has been carefully mapped and synthesized. We've drawn up a detailed original, accurate in every respect. But – '

'But it means nothing.'

The Wanderer disagreed. 'It means a great deal. But

somehow, we've failed to develop sufficient potential. Our model is static, without energy. To bridge the gap, to make it leap across, we need more power.'

Mary smiled. 'Yes. I think so.'

The Wanderer's eyes were fixed on her hungrily. 'Such power exists. I know you don't have it. But someone does; we're sure of it. It exists here, and we have to have it.'

Mary shrugged. 'What do you expect me to do?'

The gray eyes glittered. 'Tell us how to get control of Peter Trilling.'

Mary jumped in amazement. '*Peter?* He won't do you any good!'

'He has the right kind of power.'

'True. But not for your purposes. If you knew the whole story you'd understand why not.'

'Where does he get his power?'

'The same level as I.'

'That's no answer. Where does your power come from?'

'You've asked me that before,' Mary answered.

'Can't you tell us?'

'No.'

There was silence. The Wanderer drummed with her hard, blunt nails. 'It would be of considerable help to us. You know quite a lot about Peter Trilling. Why can't you tell us?'

'Don't worry,' Mary said. 'I'll take care of Peter when the time comes. Leave him to me. Actually, that part is none of your business.'

The Wanderer recoiled. 'How dare you!'

Mary laughed. 'I'm sorry. But it's the truth. I doubt if it would make your program easier if I told you about myself and Peter. It might even make it more difficult.'

'What do you know about our program? Just what we've told you.'

Mary smiled. 'Perhaps.'

There was doubt on the Wanderer's face. 'You couldn't know anymore.'

Mary got to her feet. 'Is there anything else you want to ask me?'

The Wanderer's eyes hardened. 'Have you any idea what we could do to you?'

Mary moved impatiently away. 'This is no time for nonsense. Things of great importance are happening on all sides. Instead of asking me about Peter Trilling you ought to be asking about Ted Barton.'

The Wanderer was puzzled. 'Who is Ted Barton?'

Mary pressed her small hands together and concentrated on the configuration. 'Theodore Barton is the only person to cross through the barrier in eighteen years. Except for Peter, of course. Peter comes and goes when the spirit moves him. Barton is from New York. An outsider.'

'Really?' The Wanderer was indifferent. 'I don't understand the – '

Mary dived. She missed, and it scuttled wildly off. The Wanderer quickly shut her eyes, stuck out her hands, and disappeared through the wall of the house. She was gone in an instant. Utterly silent. And Mary was alone in the darkness.

Breathing quickly, the girl scrambled through the brush, groping desperately for the tiny running figure. It couldn't go very fast; it was only three inches high. She had noticed it by chance. A sudden movement, a glint of starlight as it changed position . . .

She froze, rigid and alert, waiting for it to show itself again. It was someplace close by, probably in the heap of leaves and rotted hay piled up against the wall. Once it was past the wall and out among the trees she wouldn't have a chance of catching it. She held her breath and didn't move a muscle. They were small and agile, but stupid. Not much brighter than a mouse. But they had good memories, which mice lacked. They were excellent observers, even better than bees. They could go almost anyplace, listen and watch, and carry back letter-perfect reports. And best of all, they could be shaped in any manner, any size.

That was one thing she envied him; she had no power over clay. She was limited to bees, moths, cats and flies. The golems were invaluable; he used them all the time.

A faint sound. The golem was moving. It was in the pile of rotted hay, all right. Peeping out, wondering where she was. What a stupid golem! And like all clay things, its span of attention was incredibly short. It got restless too easily. Already, it was impatiently stirring around in the hay.

She didn't move. She remained crouched in a silent heap, palms on the ground, knees bent. Ready to spring as soon as it showed itself. She could wait as long as it could. Longer. The night was cool, but not cold. Sooner or later the golem would show itself – and that would be that.

Peter had finally overreached himself. Sent a golem too far, over the line into *her* side. *He was afraid.* The Barton man had made him uncertain. The man from outside had upset Peter's plans; he was a new element, a factor Peter didn't understand. She smiled coldly. Poor Peter. He had a surprise coming. If she was careful . . .

The golem came out. It was a male; Peter liked to form male golems. It blinked uncertainly, started off to the right, and then she had it.

It squirmed frantically inside her fist. But she didn't let go. She jumped to her feet and raced down the path, around the side of Shady House to the door.

No one saw her. The hall was empty. Her father was with some of his patients, making his eternal studies. Learning new things all the time. Devoting his life to keeping Millgate healthy.

She entered her room and carefully bolted the door. The golem was getting weak; she relaxed her muscles a little and carried it over to the table. Making certain it didn't get away, she emptied a vase of flowers into the wastebasket, then popped the vase over it. That was that. The first part was over. Now the rest. It had to be done right. She had waited a long time for this opportunity. It might never come again.

The first thing she did was take off all her clothes. She piled them neatly at the foot of the bed, as if she were in the bathroom, taking a shower. Then she got the jar of suntan oil from the medicine cabinet and carefully rubbed oil over her naked body.

It was necessary to look as much like the golem as possible. There were limitations, of course. It was a man, and she wasn't. But her body was young and unformed; her breasts were still small, not developed at all. She was slim and lithe, very much like a youth. It would do.

When every inch of her shone and glistened, she tied her long black hair up in a hard knot and wadded it tight against her neck. Actually, she should have cut it, but she didn't dare. It would take too long to grow back; there'd be questions. And anyhow, she liked it long.

What next? She examined herself. Yes, without her clothes, and her hair tied hard against the nape of her neck, she was very much like the little golem in the vase. So far so good. Lucky she wasn't older; if her breasts were any larger there wouldn't be chance. As it was, there'd be resistance; his power lay over the golem, even this far on her side of the line. It would wane in time. But the golem was undoubtedly supposed to report within the hour. She'd have to hurry; he'd begin to get suspicious.

From the medicine cabinet in the bathroom she got the three bottles and single package she needed. Rapidly, expertly, she made a dough of the powder and gums and pungent liquids, gathered it up between her fingers, and then molded an imitation golem.

Inside its vase, the real golem watched with mounting alarm. Mary laughed, and rapidly shaped the arms and legs. It was close enough; it didn't have to be too exact. She finished the feet and hands, smoothed down a few rough places, then ate it.

The dough seared her throat. She choked, tears filled her eyes. Her stomach turned over, and she caught hold of the edge of the table. The whole room was going around and around. She closed her eyes and hung on tight. Everything rolled and billowed. She knotted up as her stomach muscles writhed. Once she groaned, then managed to straighten. She took a few uncertain steps . . .

The two perspectives stunned her. And the double set of sensations. It was a long time before she dared move either body, even a trifle. On the one hand, she saw the room as it had always been; that was her own eyes and her own body. The other view was utterly strange, immense and bloated, distorted by the glass wall of the vase.

She was going to have trouble getting used to more than one body. Her own, and the one three inches high. Experimentally, she moved her smaller set of arms, then her miniature legs. She tumbled and fell; that is, the little body tumbled and fell. Her regular self stood foolishly in the center of the room, watching the whole thing.

She got up again. The wall of the vase was slippery and unpleasant. She turned her attention back to her regular self and crossed the room to the table. Carefully, she removed the vase and freed her smaller self.

For the first time in her life, she was able to see her own body from outside.

She stood still, in front of the table, while her tiny incarnation studied each inch of her. She wanted to laugh out loud; how immense she was! Huge and lumbering, a dark glowing tan. Great arms, neck, incredible moon-like face. Staring black eyes, red lips, wet white teeth.

She found it less confusing to operate each body alternately. First, she concentrated on dressing her regular body. While she put on her jeans and shirt, the little three-inch figure remained stationary. She put on her jacket and shoes, unfastened her hair and wiped the oil from her face and hands. Then she picked up the three-inch figure and placed it carefully in her breast pocket.

Strange, to be carrying herself in her own pocket. As she left the room and hurried down the hall, she was aware of the rough fabric which almost suffocated her, and the vast booming of her heart. Her breast rose and fell against her as she breathed; she was tossed around like a chip on a gigantic sea.

The night was cool. She ran quickly, through the gate and down the road. It was half a mile to town; Peter was undoubtedly at the barn, in his work chamber. Below her, Millgate stretched out, dark buildings, streets, occasional lights. In a few moments she reached the outskirts and hurried down a deserted side street. The boarding house was on Jefferson, in the center of town. The barn was just behind it.

She reached Dudley and instantly halted. Something was happening ahead of her.

She advanced cautiously. Ahead was a double line of old abandoned stores. They had rotted there for years, as long as she could remember. No one came this way anymore. The neighborhood was deserted; at least, *usually* deserted.

Two men were standing in the center of the street, a block apart. They were waving their arms and shouting back and forth at each other. Drunks, from the bars along Jefferson Street. Their voices were thick; they stumbled around clumsily. She had seen drunks wandering through the streets many times; but that wasn't what interested her.

She approached warily for a better view.

They weren't just standing there. They were doing something. Both of them were yelling and gesturing excitedly; the echoes of their noise rolled up and down the deserted streets. The two men were intent on what they were doing; they didn't notice her as she came up behind them. One of them was older, a blond-haired old man she didn't recognize. The other was Ted Barton. Recognition shocked her. What was he doing, standing in the middle of the dark street, waving his arms and shouting at the top of his lungs?

The line of rotting, deserted stores across from them looked strange. There was an eerie, insubstantial cast to it. A faint, half-visible glow had settled over the sagging roofs and porches; the broken windows were lit up by an interior light. The light seemed to excite the two men to frenzy. They ran back and forth, faster and faster, jumping and cursing and shouting.

The light increased. The old stores seemed to waver. They were fading, like an old print. Growing more and more dim even as she watched.

'Now!' the old man shrieked.

The rotting stores were going away. Fading out of existence. But something was taking their place. Something else was rapidly forming. The outlines of the stores hesitated, shifted, then dwindled rapidly. And she began to see the new shape that was emerging instead.

It wasn't stores. It was a flat surface, grass, a small building, and something else. A vague, uncertain form in the very center. Barton and his companion ran toward the form in wild excitement.

'There it is!' the old man shouted.

'You got it wrong. The barrel. It's longer.'

'No, it isn't. Come over here and concentrate on the base. Over this way.'

'What's the matter with the barrel? The barrel isn't right!'

'Of course it is. Help me with the base. And there's supposed to be a heap of cannon balls here.'

'That's right. Five or six of them.'

'And a brass plate.'

'Yes, a plate. With the name. We can't bring it back unless we have it right!'

As the two men concentrated on the rapidly forming cannon, the far edges of the park began to fade out, and a dim reminder of the stores reappeared. Barton noticed. With a wild shriek he straightened up and concentrated on the edges of the park. Waving his arms and shouting, he managed to drive the stores back out of existence. They wavered and were gone, and the extremities of the park hardened firmly.

'The path,' the old man shouted. 'Remember the path.'

'How about the benches?'

'You take care of the benches. I'll hold onto the cannon.'

'Don't forget the cannon balls!' Barton rushed off a short way, to concentrate on a bench. He ran up and down the block, forming one bench after another. In a few moments he had six or seven faded green benches, a gloomy black in the faint starlight. 'How about the flagpole?' he shouted.

'What about it?'

'Where was it? I can't remember!'

'Over this way. By the bandstand.'

'No, it wasn't. It was near the fountain. We've got to remember.'

The two of them turned their attention on another part of the park. After a moment a vague circular shape began to emerge. An ancient brass and concrete fountain. The two of them shrieked with delight. Mary gasped; water was calmly running in the fountain.

'There it is!' Barton yelled happily, waving a metal pike of some kind. 'I used to wade there. Remember? The kids used to take off their shoes and go wading.'

'Sure. I remember. How about the flagpole?'

They argued back and forth. The old man concentrated on one spot, but nothing happened. Barton concentrated on another; meanwhile, the fountain grew dim, and they had to break off abruptly and bring it back.

'Which did it have?' Barton demanded.'Which flag?'

'Both flags.'

'No, the stars and bars.'

'You're wrong. The stars and stripes.'

'I know. I'm absolutely certain!' Barton had found the spot, all right. A small concrete base and a dim, nebulous pole were rapidly forming. 'There it is!' he shouted joyfully. 'There it is!'

'Get the flag. Don't forget the flag.'

'It's night. The flag's inside.'

'That's true. There isn't any flag at night. That explains it.'

The park was almost complete. At the far edges it still wavered and faded back into the drab line of rotting old stores. But in the center it was beautifully firm and solid. The gun, the fountain, the bandstand, the benches and paths; everything was real and complete.

'We did it!' the old man shouted. He pounded Barton on the back. 'We did it!'

They hugged each other, pounded each other, embraced, then hurried deep into the park. They raced up and down the paths, around the fountain, by the cannon. His pike under his arm, Barton managed to lift one of the cannon balls; Mary could see it was terribly heavy. He dropped it with a gasp and staggered back to sit wearily down.

The two men collapsed together on one of the green benches they had summoned into being. Exhausted, they lay back, feet out, arms limp. Enjoying the satisfaction of a job well done.

Mary stepped out of the shadows and moved slowly toward them. It was time to make herself known.

# TEN

Barton saw her first. He sat up, suddenly alert, the metal tire iron drawn back. 'Who are you?' He peered at her through the gloom. Then he recognized her. 'You're one of the kids. I saw you at the boarding house.' He searched his memory. 'You're Doctor Meade's daughter.'

'That's right,' Mary said. She sat down gingerly on the bench across from them. 'May I sit on one of your benches?'

'They're not ours,' Barton answered. He was beginning to sober up. Understanding of what they had done started to trickle through his numbed brain, ice cold drops sizzling out the warmth of intoxication. 'They don't belong to us.'

'You created them, didn't you? Interesting. No one here can do that. How did you manage?'

'We didn't create them.' Barton shakily got out his cigarettes and lit up. He and Christopher glanced at each other with awe and numbed disbelief. Had they really done it? Really brought back the old park? Part of the old town?

Barton reached down and touched the bench under him. It was completely real. He was sitting on it, and so was Will Christopher. And the girl, who hadn't had anything to do with it. It wasn't a hallucination. All three of them were sitting on the benches; that was the proof.

'Well?' Christopher muttered. 'What do you think of that?'

Barton grinned shakily. 'I didn't expect such good results.'

93

The old man's eyes were wide, nostrils flaring. 'There was real ability there.' He eyed Barton with increased respect. 'You really know how to do it. You cut right through. Right to the real town.'

'It took two of us,' Barton muttered. He was cold sober, now. And exhausted. His body was utterly drained; he could hardly lift his hands. His head ached, and a nauseous taste crept up in his mouth, a sickly metallic tinge.

But they had done it.

Mary was fascinated. 'How did you do it? I've never seen something created out of nothing. Only He can do that, and even He doesn't do it anymore.'

Barton shook his head wearily. He was too tired to want to talk about it. 'Not nothing. It was there. We made it emerge.'

'Emerge?' The girl's black eyes sparkled. 'You mean those old stores were nothing but distortions?'

'Weren't really there.' Barton thumped the bench. 'This is the real thing. The real town. The other was fake.'

'What's that metal pike you're holding so tight?'

'This?' Barton turned the tire iron around. 'I brought this back. It's been a ball of string.'

Mary studied him intently. *'Is that why you came here? To bring things back?'*

It was a good question. Barton got unsteadily to his feet. 'I'm going. I've had enough for tonight.'

'Going where?' Christopher demanded.

'To my room. Have to rest. Time to think.' He tottered dopily toward the sidewalk. 'I'm exhausted. Rest and something to eat.'

Mary became instantly alert. 'You can't go near the boarding house.'

Barton blinked. 'Why the hell not?'

'Peter's there.' She leaped up and hurried after him. 'No, that's the wrong place. You want to be as far away from him as possible.'

Barton scowled. 'I'm not afraid of that punk kid. Not anymore.' He waved his tire iron menacingly.

Mary put her hand firmly on Barton's arm.

'No, it would be a big mistake to go back there. You have to go someplace else. Someplace and wait until I have this worked out. I have to understand this exactly.' She frowned, deep in thought. 'You go up to Shady House. You'll be safe up there. My father will take you in. Go right to him; don't stop and talk to anyone else. Peter won't enter that area. It's past the line.'

'The line? You mean – '

'It's on His side. You'll be safe, until I can figure this out and decide what to do. There're factors I don't understand.' She turned Barton around and impatiently pushed him the other way. 'Get going!'

She watched until she was sure they were safely across the line, on their way up the slope to Shady House. Then she hurried back toward the center of town.

She had to move fast. Time was running out. Peter was undoubtedly suspicious, looking for his golem and wondering why it wasn't back.

She patted her pocket gently and, at the same time, felt the great mass of rough cloth billow against her. She still hadn't got used to being in two places at once; as soon as the golem had done its work she'd leave it as she had found it.

Jefferson Street loomed ahead. She ran rapidly down it, black hair streaming behind her, breasts heaving. With one hand she held her pocket; it would be too bad to let her little self fall out and get destroyed.

There was the boarding house. A few people were on the porch, enjoying the coolness and darkness. She turned up the driveway and scampered around back, across the field, toward the barn. There it was, the vast, ominous shape rising up against the night sky. She crouched in the shadows behind a shrub to get her breath and size up the situation.

Peter was certainly inside. Up in his work chamber with his cages and jars and urns of moist clay. She glanced hopefully around; was there a night-flying moth she could send in? She saw none, and anyhow, they didn't have a chance.

Carefully, with gentle fingers, she opened her pocket and got out her three-inch self. Sudden vision took the place of endless rough fabric. She closed her regular eyes and put herself as much as possible in the golem. Now she felt her own massive hand, her giant fingers touching her – too roughly, too.

By moving her attention from one body to the other she was able to manipulate the golem-self onto the ground and several feet in the direction of the barn. Almost at once it was in the interference zone.

She made her regular body sit down in the shadows, bend over in a heap, knees drawn up, head down, arms clasped around its ankles. That way she could concentrate all her attention on the golem.

The golem passed through the interference zone un-noticed. It warily approached the barn. There was a little golem-ladder Peter had rigged up. She peered around, trying to find it. The side of the barn reared, immense rough boards, towering up to lose themselves in the black sky. A structure so large she couldn't make out its extreme dimensions.

She found the ladder. Several spiders passed her, as she

awkwardly climbed it. They were descending hurriedly to ground level. And once, a host of gray rats scurried past her at an excited rate.

She ascended cautiously. Below, among the bushes and vines, snakes rustled. Peter had all his things out tonight. The situation must have really disturbed him. She found the entrance steps and left the ladder. A hole, a black tunnel, lay ahead. And beyond it, a light. She was there. The night-flyers had never penetrated this far. This was Peter's work chamber.

For a moment the golem paused. Mary let it stand at the entrance of the hole while she turned her attention briefly back to her regular body. Already, the regular body was getting stiff and chill. It was a cold night; she couldn't sit there on the ground, in the shadows.

She stretched her arms and legs, knotted and unknotted her muscles. The golem might be inside the barn a long time. She'd have to find a place to stay. Maybe one of the all-night cafes on Jefferson Street. She could sit drinking hot coffee until the golem had done its business. Maybe have some hot-cakes and syrup, read a discarded newspaper and listen to the jukebox.

She moved cautiously through the bushes, toward the field. The cold made her shiver and pull her jacket around her. Having two bodies was fun, but it was really too much trouble to be worth . . .

Something dropped on her. She brushed it quickly off. A spider, from the tree above.

More spiders fell. A sharp pain seared across her cheek. She leaped wildly and slapped at it. A whole torrent of gray swarmed through the bushes and across her feet, up her jeans and over her body.

Rats. Spiders fell on her neck and shoulders in great heaps, into her hair, down the front of her shirt. She shrieked and struggled frantically. More rats; they sank their yellow teeth into her silently. She began to run, blindly, in aimless panic. The rats followed; they hung onto her. More leaped to catch hold. Spiders scurried over her face, between her breasts, into her armpits.

She stumbled and fell. Vines caught at her. More rats threw themselves on her. Swarms of them. Spiders fell soundlessly on all sides. She writhed and fought; her whole body was alive with pain. Gummy webs draped across her face and eyes, choked her and blinded her.

She struggled to her knees, crawled a few feet, then sank down under the load of biting, gnawing creatures. They burrowed into her, dug for her bones, through her skin and flesh. They were eating her body away. She screamed and screamed but the web-stuff choked her voice off. Spiders swarmed into her mouth, her nose, everywhere.

Rustles from the dark bushes. She felt, rather than saw, the glittery twisting bodies come spiraling toward her. By that time she had no eyes, nothing to see with and no way to scream. It was the end, and she knew it.

She was already dead, as the copperheads slid moistly over her prone body, and sank their fangs into unresisting flesh.

# ELEVEN

'Stand still!' Doctor Meade ordered sharply. 'And don't make any noise.'

He emerged from the shadows behind them, a grim figure in his long overcoat and hat. Barton and Christopher halted warily, as he came up behind them, a massive .45 clutched in his fist. Barton let the tire iron hang loosely, ready for anything.

Shady House loomed up ahead. The front door was open. Many windows were yellow squares; the patients were still awake. The large fenced-in yard was dark and gloomy. The cedars at the edge of the hill swayed and rustled with the cold night wind.

'I was in my station wagon,' Doctor Meade said. 'I saw you coming up the slope.' He flashed his flashlight in Barton's face. 'I remember you. You're the man from New York. What are you doing here?'

Barton found his voice. 'Your daughter told us to come up here.'

Meade instantly stiffened. 'Mary? *Where is she?* I was out looking for her. She left half an hour ago. There's something going on.' He hesitated, then decided. 'Come inside,' he ordered, putting his gun away.

They followed him down the yellow-lit corridor, down a flight of stairs to his office. Meade locked the door and pulled down the blinds. He pushed aside a microscope and a heap of charts and papers, then seated himself on the corner of his coffee-stained oak desk.

'I was driving around looking for Mary. I passed along

Dudley.' Meade's shrewd eyes bored into Barton. 'I saw a park on Dudley. It wasn't there before. It wasn't there this morning. Where'd it come from? What happened to the old stores?'

'You're wrong,' Barton said. 'The park was there before. Eighteen years ago.'

Doctor Meade licked his lips. 'Interesting. Do you know where my daughter is?'

'Not now. She sent us up here and went on.'

There was silence. Doctor Meade peeled off his overcoat and hat and tossed them over a chair. 'So you brought the park back, did you?' he said finally. 'One of you must have a good memory. The Wanderers have tried repeatedly and failed.'

Barton sucked in his breath. 'You mean – '

'They know there's something wrong. They've mapped out the whole town. They go out every night, with their eyes shut. Back and forth. Getting every detail of the understrata. But no dice; they're lacking something vital.'

'They go out with their eyes shut? *Why?*'

'So the distortion won't affect them. They can bypass the distortion, all right. But as soon as they open their eyes it's all back. The fake town. They know it's only an illusion, an imposed layer. But they can't get rid of it.'

'Why not?'

Meade smiled. '*Because they're distorted themselves.* They were all here when the Change came.'

'Who are the Wanderers?' Barton demanded.

'People of the old town.'

'I thought so.'

'People who weren't completely altered by the Change. It missed a number of them. The Change came and left them more or less unaffected. It varies.'

'Like me,' Christopher murmured.

Meade eyed him. 'Yes, you're a Wanderer. With a little practice you could learn to bypass the distortion and nightwalk, like the others. But that would be all. You couldn't bring the old town back. You're distorted to some degree, every one of you.' His eyes were on Barton as he continued slowly, 'None of you has a perfect memory.'

'I have,' Barton said, understanding his look. 'I wasn't here. I left before the Change.'

Doctor Meade said nothing. But his expression was enough.

'Where can I find the Wanderers?' Barton asked tersely.

'They're everywhere,' Meade answered evasively. 'Haven't you seen them?'

'They must start out someplace. They must have organized themselves together in a particular location.'

The doctor's heavy face twisted in indecision. An internal struggle was going on. 'What happens when you find them?' he demanded.

'Then we reconstruct the old town. As it was. As it still is, underneath.'

'You'll throw off the distortion?'

'If we can.'

Meade nodded slowly. 'You can, Barton. *Your* memory is unimpaired. Once you get hold of the Wanderers' maps you'll be able to correct – ' He broke off. 'Let me ask you this. Why do you want to bring back the old town?'

Barton was appalled. 'Because it's the real town! All these people, houses, stores, are illusions. The real town's buried underneath.'

'Did it ever occur to you that maybe some of these people prefer the illusion?'

For a moment Barton didn't understand. Then it came to him. 'Good God,' he whispered softly.

Doctor Meade turned away. 'That's right. I'm one of the distortions, not a Wanderer. I didn't exist before the Change; not like I am now. And I don't want to go back.'

The thing was rapidly clearing for Barton. 'And not just you. Your daughter, Mary. She was born since the Change. And Peter. His mother. Miss James. The man in the hardware store. All of them. They're all distortions.'

'Just you and me,' Christopher said to him. 'We're the only real ones.'

'And the Wanderers.' Barton let his breath out in a rush. 'I see your point. But you did exist *in some form* before the Change. There was something; you didn't come out of nothing.'

Meade's heavy features were gray with pain. 'Of course. But *what*? Look, Barton. I've known for years about this. Known this town, all these people, were imitations. Fakes. But goddammit, I'm part of this distortion. I'm afraid. I like it this way. I have my work. My hospital here, my daughter. I get along well with the people.'

'The imitation people.'

Meade's lips twisted miserably. 'Like it says in the Bible, "We see as through a glass, darkly." But how does it hurt me? Maybe I was worse off, before. I don't know!'

'You don't know anything about your life before the Change?' Barton was puzzled. 'Can't the Wanderers tell you anything?'

'They don't know. There's a lot they don't remember.' Meade raised his eyes imploringly. 'I've tried to find some clue, but there's nothing. No trace.'

'There'll be others like him,' Christopher said. 'A lot of them won't want to go back.'

'What did it?' Barton demanded. 'Why did the Change come?'

'I don't understand much of it,' Meade answered. 'A contest, a struggle of some kind. With rules. One hand tied behind the back. *And something got in.* Forced its way into this valley. Eighteen years ago it found the weak place. A crack through which it could enter. It's always tried, eternally. The two of them, eternal conflict. *He* built all this – this world. And then it took advantage of the rules. Came through and changed everything.'

'I have a good idea.' Meade crossed to the window and let up the blind. 'If you look you'll see them. They're always there. They never move. One at each end. He's over this way. And at the other – *it*.'

Barton looked out. The shapes were still there, as Meade said. Exactly as he had seen them from Peter's ledge.

'He comes from the sun,' Meade said.

'Yes. I saw him at midday. His head was one vast ball of shining light.'

'*It* comes from cold and darkness. They've always existed. I've pieced together things, here and there. But there's so much I don't know. This struggle here is only a small part of it. A microscopic section. They fight everywhere. All over the universe. That's what the universe is for. So they'll have a place to do battle.'

'A battleground,' Barton murmured. The window faced the side of darkness. *Its* side, bleak and frigid. He could see it standing there. Immense. No limit to it. The thing's head was lost in space. The numbing emptiness of deep space. Where there was no life, no being, no existence. Only silence and eternal wastes.

And He – from the boiling suns. The hot flaming masses of gas that bubbled and hurled up streamers and ignited the darkness. Fiery shafts that penetrated the void, reaching, groping, pushing back the cold. Filling the emptiness with hot sound and motion. An eternal struggle. Sterile darkness, silence, cold, immobility, death, on one hand. And on the other, the flaming heat of life. Blinding suns, birth and generation, awareness and being.

The cosmic polarities.

'He is Ormazd,' Doctor Meade said.

'And it?'

'Out of darkness, filth and death. Chaos and evil. Seeking to destroy His law. His order and truth. Its ancient name is Ahriman.'

Barton was silent a moment. 'I suppose Ormazd will win, eventually.'

'According to the legend, He will triumph and absorb Ahriman. The struggle has gone on billions of years. It will certainly go on several billions more.'

'Ormazd the builder,' Barton said. 'Ahriman the wrecker.'

'Yes,' Meade said.

'The old town is Ormazd's. Ahriman laid this layer of black fog, this distortion and illusion.'

Meade hesitated. 'Yes.'

Barton tensed himself; it was now or never. 'Where can we make contact with the Wanderers?'

Meade struggled violently. 'I – ' He started to answer, then changed his mind. His face sagged into gray decision. 'I can't tell you, Barton. If there were some way I could stay as I am, keep my daughter as she is . . .'

There was a brisk knock on the door. 'Doctor, let me in,' a woman's voice came sharply. 'Important news.'

Meade scowled furiously. 'One of my patients.' He unbolted the door impatiently and slid it aside a crack. 'What the hell do you want?'

A young woman pushed quickly into the room. Blonde-haired, thin-faced, pale cheeks flushed. 'Doctor, your daughter is dead. We were informed by a night-flying death's-head. She was caught and destroyed on the other side of the line. Just beyond the neutral zone, near his work chamber.'

Meade shuddered; both Barton and Christopher reacted violently. Barton felt his heart come to a complete stop. The girl was dead. Peter had murdered her. But it was something else that made him move quickly to the door and slam it shut. The last piece had fitted in place, and he didn't want to waste any time.

The young woman, Doctor Meade's patient, was one of the pair of Wanderers who had moved through the porch of the Trilling boarding house. He had finally found them, and it was about time.


Peter Trilling kicked at the remains with his foot. The rats were feeding noisily. Quarreling and fighting and snapping at each other greedily. He pondered a while, a little dazed by the suddenness of it. After a time he wandered aimlessly away, arms folded, deep in thought.

The golems were excited. And the spiders didn't want to go back to their jars. They buzzed and scurried all around him, gathered on his face and hands, raced after him. Countless faint whines pierced his ears, a growing chatter of golem and rat restlessness. They sensed a major victory had occurred; they were eager for more.

He picked up a copperhead and automatically stroked its sleek sides. *She was dead.* In a single swift stroke the whole balance of power had changed. He dropped the snake and increased his pace. He was approaching Jefferson Street and the main part of town. His mind raced in wild turmoil; thoughts came faster and faster. Was this really the time? Had the moment finally come?

He turned to face the far wall of the valley, the towering ring of mountains against the black sky. There it was. Standing there, arms out, feet apart, its head an infinite sheet of black emptiness that stretched eternally, a universe of silence and quietude.

The sight of it sent the last traces of doubt from him. He turned and started back toward his work chamber, suddenly eager and impatient.

A group of golems hurried excitedly to him, all clamoring for his attention. More streaked toward him from the center of town. They were terribly upset; their piping voices echoed as they swarmed up his clothing.

They wanted him to see something. They were afraid. Angrily, he followed them back into the town. Down dark streets, past rows of silent houses. What did they want? What were they trying to show him?

At Dudley Street they halted. Ahead, something glimmered and glowed. For a time he couldn't see what it was. Something was happening, but what? A lapping flame, low and intense, played over buildings and stores, telephone poles, the pavement itself. Curious, he made his way forward.

A shapeless mass lay on the pavement. He bent down uneasily. Clay. An inert lump of clay. There were others, all dead and unmoving. Cold. He picked one up in his hands.

It was a golem. Or what had once been a golem. It was no longer alive. Incredibly, it had been returned to its primordial state of non-existence. It was dead clay again. The clay from which it had been formed. Dry and shapeless and totally lifeless. It had been ungolemed.

Such a thing had never happened before. His still-living

106

golems retreated in horror; they were terrified by the sight of their inert brethren. This was what he had been called to see.

Peter moved forward, perplexed. The light played ahead. The lapping fire that crept and crawled from building to building. Spreading out silently. A growing circle that widened each moment. There was a strange intensity about it. A determined quality. It missed nothing. Like burning water it advanced and absorbed everything.

In the center was a park. Paths, benches and an ancient gun. A flagpole. A building.

He had never seen it before. There was no park here! What did it mean? What had happened to the rows of deserted stores?

He swept up all the still-living golems and squeezed their struggling, piping bodies together in a common mass. The ball of living clay twisted, as he rapidly reformed it. From the mass he fashioned a head, without a body. Eyes, nose, then mouth, tongue, teeth, palate, and lips. He set it down on the pavement and pressed the edges of the neck until it stood.

'When did this begin?' he demanded.

The lips moved, as the several minds summoned their memories. 'An hour ago,' it croaked finally.

'Those who were ungolemed! How did it happen? Who did it?'

'They entered the park. They tried to pass through it.'

'And it ungolemed them?'

'They came out slowly. They were weak. Then they lay down and died. We were afraid to go near.'

It was true, then. The spreading circle had done it. He pushed the features of the head back into shapelessness, then stuffed the clay into his pockets. The clay squirmed against his legs, each bit alive. Peter got cautiously to his feet. The circle of fire had expanded; it moved constantly. Taking in more and more buildings. Soundlessly increasing. It was highly unstable. A menace to everything close by.

And then he understood.

It wasn't destroying. It was changing things. As the buildings and houses sank down into the fire, other shapes emerged to take their places. Other forms, rising up from the lapping glow. Objects he had never seen before. Shapes unfamiliar. Alien to him.

For a long time he stood watching, while his golems flitted about him nervously, plucking at him and trying to make him leave. The fire advanced near; Peter took a few steps back.

He was excited. Joy and wild exhilaration burst loose inside him. The time had arrived. Her death – and now this. The balance had swung. The line no longer signified anything.

This, the restorer. Primordial shapes, rising from beneath. Springing back into being, from the depths below. The last element. The final piece needed.

He made his decision. Quickly, he emptied his pockets of the squirming clay, took a deep, shuddering breath, and crouched. For a last time he glanced back and up, at the towering shapes of darkness jutting against the sky. The sight filled him with strength – the strength he was going to need.

He ran straight into the lapping tongues of fire.

# TWELVE

The Wanderers watched intently as Barton corrected the last of the maps.

'This is wrong,' he muttered. He struck out a whole street with his pencil. 'This was Lawton Avenue here. And you've got most of the houses wrong.' He concentrated. 'A small bakery was here. With a green sign over it. Owned by a man named Oliver.' He pulled the name-chart over and ran his finger along it. 'You've missed it here, too.'

Christopher stood behind him, peering over his shoulder. 'Wasn't there a young girl working there? I seem to remember a heavy-set girl. Glasses, thick legs. A niece or something. Julia Oliver.'

'That's right.' Barton finished the correction. 'At least twenty percent of your reconstruction schematics is inaccurate. Our work with the park showed us we had to be letter-perfect.'

'Don't forget the big old brown house,' Christopher put in excitedly. 'There was a dog there, a little short-haired terrier. Bit me on the ankle.' He reached down and felt around. 'The scar went away on the day of the Change.' A strange look crossed his face. 'I'm sure I was bit there. Maybe – '

'You probably were,' Barton said. 'I remember a short-haired Spitz on that street. I'll put it in.'

Doctor Meade stood in the corner of the room, grief-stricken and dazed. Wanderers swarmed around the long drafting table, carrying charts and maps and data sheets back and forth. The whole building hummed with activity. All the Wanderers were there, in their bathrobes and slippers, two-piece gray pajamas. Excited and alert, now that the time had finally come.

Barton got up and approached Doctor Meade. 'You knew all the time. That's why you collected them here.'

Meade nodded. 'As many as I could locate. I missed Christopher.'

'Why did you do it?'

Meade's agonized features twisted. 'They don't belong down there. And – '

'And what?'

'And I knew they were the right ones. I found them wandering aimlessly around Millgate. Random. Meaningless. Thinking they were lunatics. I brought them together up here.'

'But that's all. You won't do anymore.'

Meade futilely clenched and unclenched his fists. 'I should have acted. I should have thrown my weight against the boy. He's going to suffer, Barton. I'll make him suffer in ways he knows nothing about.'

Barton returned to the drafting table. Hilda, the leader of the Wanderers, called him urgently over to her desk. 'We've got them fairly well corrected. You're sure about all these alterations? You're not in doubt?'

'I'm sure.'

'You must understand. Our own memories are vague, impaired. Not sharp like your own. At best we remember only dim snatches of the town before the Change.'

'You were lucky to get out,' a young woman murmured, studying Barton intently.

'We saw the park,' another said, a gray-haired man with thick glasses. 'We were never able to do that.'

Another tapped his cigarette thoughtfully. 'None of us

110

has a really clear memory. Only you, Barton. You're the only one.'

There was tension in the room. All the Wanderers had stopped work. They had drawn around Barton in a taut ring. Tense men and women. Earnest and deadly serious.

The whole side of the room was taken up with files. Heaps of charts and reports, endless stacks of data and records. Typewriters, pencils, reams of paper, cards, reference photos tacked on the walls. Graphs, detailed studies, bound and well-thumbed. Tables of ceramic materials. The actual three-dimensional model. Paints, brushes, pigments, glues and drawing equipment. Slide rules, measuring tape, cutting pliers, hacksaws.

The Wanderers had been working a long time. There weren't many of them; out of the whole town they were a small group. But their faces showed their determination. They had staked a lot on their work. They weren't going to let anything jeopardize it.

'I'm going to ask you something,' Hilda said carefully. Between her competent fingers her cigarette burned unnoticed. 'You say you left Millgate in 1935. When you were a child. Is that right?'

Barton nodded. 'That's right.'

'And you've been gone all this time?'

'Yes.'

A low murmur moved through the room. Barton felt uneasy. He tightened his hold on the tire iron and waited.

'You know,' Hilda continued, choosing her words carefully, 'that a barrier has been put across the highway, two miles outside of town.'

'I know,' Barton said.

All eyes were on Barton as Hilda continued calmly. 'Then how did you get back into the valley? The barrier seals us all in here. And it seals everyone else out.'

'That's right,' Barton admitted.

'You must have had help getting in.' Abruptly, Hilda stubbed out her cigarette. 'Somebody with superior power. *Who was it?*'

'I don't know.'

A Wanderer got to his feet. 'Throw him out. Or better yet – '

'Wait.' Hilda raised her hand menacingly. 'Barton, we've worked years to build all this. We can't take chances. You may have been sent here to help us, and maybe not. We know only one thing for certain. *You're not on your own*. You had help, assistance from someone. And you're still under superior control.'

'Yes,' Barton agreed wearily. 'I had help. I was brought here, let past the barrier. And I'm probably still being manipulated. But I don't know any more than that.'

'Kill him,' a slim, brown-haired Wanderer said. She glanced up mildly. 'It's the only way to be sure. If he can't tell us whose agent he is – '

'Nonsense!' a plump, middle-aged man retorted. 'He brought back the park, didn't he? And he corrected our maps.'

'Corrected?' Hilda's eyes were bleak. 'Changed, perhaps. How do we know they were corrected?'

Barton licked his dry lips. 'Look,' he began. 'What am I supposed to say? If I don't know who brought me here I sure as hell can't tell you.'

Doctor Meade moved between Barton and Hilda. 'Shut up and listen to me,' he grated. 'Both of you.' His voice was hard and urgent. 'Barton can't tell anybody anything. Maybe he's a plant, sent here to break you. It's possible. He may be a creation, a super-golem. There's no way to tell, not now. Later on, when reconstruction begins. If it really works you'll know. But not now.'

'Then,' the slim, brown-haired girl observed, 'it'll be too late.'

Meade agreed grimly. 'Yes, much too late. Once you start the fat's in the fire. You won't be able to back out. If Barton's a plant you're finished.' He smiled humorlessly. 'Even Barton doesn't know what he's going to do, when the time comes.'

'What are you getting at?' a thin, sallow-faced Wanderer demanded.

Meade's answer was directly to the point. 'You'll have to take a chance on him, whether you like it or not. You have no choice. He's the only one who's been able to reconstruct. He brought back a whole park in half an hour. You haven't been able to do a damn thing in eighteen years.'

There was stunned silence.

'You're impotent,' Meade continued. 'All of you. You were all here. You're like me, distorted. *But he's not.* You'll have to trust him. Either take a chance or sit here with your useless maps until you die of old age.'

For a long time no one said anything. The Wanderers sat rigid, faces shocked.

'Yes,' the slim, brown-haired girl said finally. She pushed her coffee cup aside and leaned back in her chair. 'He's right. We don't have a choice.'

Hilda looked from one to the next, around the circle of gray-clad men and women. She saw the same look on all their faces. Hopeless resignation.

'All right,' she said. 'Then let's get moving. The sooner the better. I doubt if we have much time.'

The board fences were quickly knocked down. The surface of the rise was cleared; cedars cut down, bushes cleared away. All obstructions removed. In an hour, there was a clear view of the valley, and the town of Millgate below.

Barton moved uneasily around, swinging his tire iron. Maps and charts were carefully laid out. Detailed, letter-perfect schematics of the old town; every factor had been added and entered in its proper place. The Wanderers organized themselves in a circle around the charts, a closed ring facing inward. Up and down the slope fluttered night-flyers, huge gray moths bringing news up from the valley, and carrying messages back and forth.

'We're limited at night,' Hilda said to Barton. 'The bees are no good, and the flies are too dulled and stupefied.'

'You mean you can't be certain what's going on down there?'

'Frankly, no. Moths are unreliable. As soon as the sun comes up we'll have the bees. There's much better results to be obtained – '

'What do they say about Peter?'

'Nothing. No reports on him at all. They've lost him.' She looked worried. 'They say he disappeared. All at once, without warning. No further sign.'

'Would they know if he crossed over here?'

'If he came, he'd be protected. Spinners to handle the night-flyers would spread out in advance. They're terrified of the spinners. And he's bred hundreds of them in his work chamber. Bottles of them, just for this.'

'What else can we count on?'

'Some cats may show up. But there's absolutely no organization there. Whatever they feel like – no more. If they want to they'll come. Otherwise we can't force them. Only the bees can really be counted on. And they won't be up for another couple of hours.'

Below, the lights of Millgate flickered dully in the early-morning darkness. Barton examined his wristwatch.

It was three-thirty A.M. Cold and dark, the sky overcast with a moist layer of ominous mist. He didn't like the look of things. The night-flyers had lost Peter; he was on the move. He'd already killed the girl. He was damn clever, to shake the night-flyers at a time like this. And he was after Barton's hide.

'How does he fit into all this?' Barton demanded.

'Peter?' Hilda shook her head. 'We don't know. He has tremendous power, but we've never been able to approach him. Mary handled him. She had power, too. We never understood either of them. We Wanderers are ordinary people. Doing that best we can to get our town back.'

The circle was ready to begin the first attempt to lift the distortion layer. Barton took his place and was quickly linked with the others. All faces were turned toward the maps spread out on the ground, faintly moist with night dew. Star-light filtered down on them, diffused by the billowing mist.

'These maps,' Hilda said, 'are to be considered adequate symbols of the territory below. For this attempt we must use the basic principle of M-kinetics: *the symbolic representation is identical with the object represented*. If the symbol is accurate, it can be considered the object itself. Any difference between them is purely logical.'

M-kinetics, the correct term for the archaic, timeless processes of magic. The manipulation of real objects through symbolic or verbal representations. The charts of Millgate were related to the town itself; because they were perfectly drawn, any force affecting the charts would affect the town. Like a wax doll molded to resemble a person, the charts had been constructed to resemble the town. If the resemblance were perfect, failure was impossible.

115

'Here we go,' Hilda said quietly. She motioned, and the model team entered the first three-dimensional section on the schematic map.

Barton sat moodily at his place, tapping the tire iron against the ground and watching the teams building up the schematics into a perfect miniature of the old town. Rapidly, one house after another was constructed, painted and finished, then pushed into place. But his heart wasn't in it. He was thinking about Mary. And wondering with growing uneasiness what Peter Trilling was up to.

The first reports from night-flyers began to filter in. As Hilda listened to the ring of moths dancing and fluttering around her, the harsh lines of her mouth hardened. 'Not so good,' she said to Barton.

'What's wrong?'

'We're not getting the results we should.'

An uneasy murmur moved through the circle of Wanderers. More and more buildings, streets, stores, houses, minute men and women, were pushed into place, an accelerating program of nervous activity.

'We'll bypass the Dudley Street area,' Hilda ordered. 'Barton's re-creation has spread over three or four blocks, now. Most of that region is already restored.'

Barton blinked. 'How come?'

'As people see the old park, it recalls awareness of the old town. By cracking the distortion layer in a single place you started a chain of reaction that should eventually spread through the whole imitation town.'

'Maybe that'll be enough.'

'Normally it would be. But something's wrong.' Hilda turned her head to hear a new series of reports being brought up the slope by relay night-flyers. Her expression of concern deepened. 'This is bad,' she murmured.

'What is it?' Barton demanded.

'According to the late information, your circle of recreation has ceased growing. It's been neutralized.'

Barton was appalled. 'You mean we're being stopped? Something's working against us?'

Hilda didn't answer. A whole flock of excited gray moths was fluttering around her head. She turned away from Barton to catch what they were saying.

'It's getting more serious,' she said, when the moths had fluttered off again.

Barton didn't have to hear. He could tell by her face what it was. 'Then we might as well quit,' he said thickly. 'If it's that bad . . .'

Christopher hurried over. 'What's happening? Isn't it working?'

'We're meeting opposition,' Barton answered. 'They've succeeded in neutralizing our zone of reconstruction.'

'Worse,' Hilda said calmly. 'Something has sucked up our M-energy. The zone has begun to shrink.' A faint smile, ironic and mirthless, touched her lips briefly. 'We took a chance. We gambled on you, Barton. And we lost. Your lovely park isn't holding its own. It's nice, but it isn't permanent. They're rolling us back.'

# THIRTEEN

Barton got unsteadily to his feet and moved away from the circle. Moths fluttered around him, as he felt his way through the half-darkness, along the side of the slope, hands deep in the pockets of his rumpled gray suit.

They were losing. The reconstruction attempt had failed.

Far off, at the other end of the valley, he could make out the great bleak figure of Ahriman. The giant shape against the night sky, arms outstretched over them all, the cosmic wrecker. Where the hell was Ormazd? Barton craned his neck and tried to look straight up. Ormazd was supposed to be *here*; this ridge was about even with His kneecap. Why didn't He do something? What was holding Him back?

Below, the lights of the town winked. The fake town, the distortion Ahriman had cast, eighteen years ago, the day of the Change. The day Ormazd's great original plan had been monkeyed with, while He did nothing. Why did He let Ahriman get away with it? Didn't He care what happened to His design? Didn't it interest Him?

'It's an old problem,' Doctor Meade said, from the shadows. 'If God made the world, where did Evil come from . . .'

'He just stands there,' Barton said futilely. 'Like a big carved rock. While we try like hell to fix things up the way He had them. You'd think He'd give us a hand.'

'His ways are strange.'

'You don't seem to care particularly.'

118

'I care. I care so much I can't talk about it.'

'Maybe your chance will come.'

'I hope so.' After a moment Meade said, 'It isn't going well.'

'No. We're washed up. I guess I didn't turn out to be much help. The crisis has come and I can't do anything.'

'Why not?'

'Not enough power. Somebody's moving between our model and the object. Cutting us off. Rolling the reconstructed area back.'

'Who?'

'You know.' Barton indicated the slope and the town below. 'He's down there, somewhere. With his rats and spiders and snakes.'

Meade's hands twisted. 'If I could get my hands on him . . .'

'You had your chance. You were happy with things as they are.'

'Barton, I was afraid. I didn't want to go back to my old form.' Meade's eyes were pleading. 'I'm still afraid. I know this is all wrong; don't you think I understand that? But I can't do it. I can't face going back. I don't know why. I don't even know what I was. Barton, I'm actually *glad* it's failing. You understand? I'm glad it's going to stay the way it is. God, I wish I were dead.'

Barton wasn't listening. He was watching something half way down the side of the slope.

In the gloom, a gray cloud was moving slowly upward. It heaved and surged, a billowing mass that grew larger each moment. What was it? He couldn't make it out, in the half-light of early morning. Nearer and nearer the cloud came. Some of the Wanderers had broken away from the circle and were hurrying uneasily to the edge of the slope. From the cloud, a low murmur came. A distant drumming.

119

Moths.

A few gray shapes fluttered wildly past Barton, toward Hilda. A vast solid mass of death's-head moths, pushing in panic up the slope toward the Wanderers. Thousands of them. All were there, the whole bunch from the valley floor. Returning in a mass. But why?

And then he saw. At the same time, the rest of the Wanderers broke away from the circle and flocked to the edge of the slope. Hilda shouted quick, frantic orders. Reconstruction was forgotten. All of them grouped together, whitefaced and terrified. The fleeing moths broke over them in panic-stricken waves, useless remnants without order or direction.

A bit of spider's web drifted around Barton. He plucked it away. A thick mass of web blew against his face; he tore it quickly away. Now the spiders themselves were visible. Hopping and hurrying through the brush, up the side of the slope. Like rising gray water, a furry tide, lapping from rock to rock. Gaining speed as they came.

And after them, the rats. Scurrying shapes that rustled dryly, countless glittering red eyes, yellow fangs twitching. He couldn't see past them. But someplace beyond were the snakes. Or maybe the snakes had come around the other way. Probably they were creeping and slithering up from behind. It made sense.

A Wanderer shrieked, stumbled back and collapsed. Something tiny and energetic leaped from it and onto the next figure. The Wanderer shook it off, then stepped down hard. A golem. Something flashed wicked white to the night gloom.

He had armed his golems.

It was going to be ugly. Barton retreated with the other Wanderers, away from the edge. The golems had come around the sides; nobody had seen them. The moths cared about the spiders and nothing else; they hadn't even noticed the running, leaping figures of animated clay. A whole pack of golems dashed toward Hilda. She fought wildly, stepped on some, tore others apart with her hands, smashed another as it tried to climb toward her face.

Barton hurried over and crushed a pack of golems with his tire iron. The rest scurried off. Hilda shuddered and half fell; he caught hold of her. Needles were sticking from her arms and legs, microscopic spears the golems had left. 'They're all around here,' Barton grunted. 'We don't have a chance.'

'Where'll we go? Down to the floor?'

Barton looked quickly around. The tide of spiders had already poured over the lip of the ridge. In a moment the rats would be along. Something crunched under his foot. He recoiled. The cold body of a snake moving toward Hilda. Barton retched with disgust and kept moving.

They had to keep moving. Back toward the house. Wanderers were fighting on all sides, kicking and stepping and struggling with closing rings of yellow-toothed shadows and leaping three-inch figures with glittering swords. The spiders weren't really much good; they had scared off the moths and that was about all. But the snakes . . .

A Wanderer went down under a pile of gnawing gray. Rats and golems together. Things of dust and old hair and dry filth. He could see better; the sky had turned from deep violet to stark white. In a while the sun would be coming up.

Something stabbed into Barton's leg. He smashed the golem in half with his tire iron and moved back. They were everywhere. Rats were clinging to his trouser cuffs. Up and down his arms furry spiders scrambled, trying to get webs around him. He broke away and retreated.

A shape appeared ahead. At first he thought it was one

of the Wanderers. It wasn't. It had come up the slope with the horde. Slowly and awkwardly, trailing after them. It was in charge. But it wasn't used to climbing.

Momentarily, he forgot the rats and golems biting at him. Nothing he had seen so far had prepared him for this. It took a while for him to comprehend, and then it almost swept his mind away.

He had been expecting Peter, of course. Wondering when he would show up. But Peter had been down on the valley floor. He had been touched by the reconstruction, by the growing area of the park.

Peter was formed after the Change. What Barton had known was only the distorted shape. The thing weaving and quivering in front of him had been Peter. That was its false shape, and that false shape was gone. This was its real shape. It had been reconstructed.

It was Ahriman.

Everyone was scattering. All the Wanderers were fleeing toward Shady House in crazed panic. Hilda disappeared from sight, cut off by a slithering carpet of gray. Christopher was fighting his way free, with a group of Wanderers, near the door of the house. Doctor Meade had forced his way to his car and was trying to get the door open. Some of the others had got into Shady House and were barricading themselves in their rooms. Useless last-ditch fights, each of them cut off, isolated from the others. To be torn down, one by one.

Barton crushed golems and rats underfoot as he retreated, his tire iron swinging furiously. Ahriman was huge. In the shape of a human boy it had been small, cut down to size. Now there was no holding it. Even as he watched, it grew. A bubbling, swelling mass of gray-yellow jelly. Particles of filth embedded in it. A tangled web of thick hair, clotted and dripping as the thing dragged itself forward. The hair quivered and twitched, sprouted and extended itself in all directions. Bits of the thing were deposited down the slope, the way it had come. Like a cosmic slug it left a trail of slime and offal as it went.

It fed constantly. It was bloating itself on the things it caught. Its tentacles swept up Wanderers, golems, rats, and snakes indiscriminately. He could see a rubbish-heap of cadavers littered through its jelly, in all stages of decomposition. It swept up and absorbed everything, all life, whatever it touched. It turned life into a barren path of filth and ruin and death.

Ahriman took in life and breathed out the numbing, barren chill of deep space. A frigid, biting wind. The blight of death and emptiness. A sickening odor, a rancid stench. Its natural smell. Decay and corruption and death. And it continued to grow. Soon it would be too big for the valley. Too big for the world.

Barton ran. He leaped over a double line of golems and raced between trees, giant cedars growing by the side of Shady House.

Spiders fell on him in torrents. He swept them off and hurried blindly on. Aimlessly. Behind him the towering shape of Ahriman grew. It wasn't exactly moving. It had stopped at the edge of the slope and anchored itself. Writhing and twisting, it jutted up higher and higher, a mountain of filth and bubbling jelly. And as it grew, its cold chill settled over everything.

Barton halted, gasping for breath and getting his bearings. He was in a hollowed-out place beyond the cedars, just above the road. The whole valley, in its early-morning beauty, was emerging from the darkness beneath him. But over the fields and farms and houses a vast shadow was falling. More intense than the one lifting. The shadow of

Ahriman, as the destroyer-god expanded to its regular proportions. And this shadow would never lift.

Something slithered. A shiny-backed body lashed at Barton. He twisted away frantically. The copperhead missed, drew back to strike again. Barton hurled his tire iron. It caught the snake dead center and crushed its back into a pulp.

He snatched up the iron just in time. Snakes were everywhere. He had come across a whole nest of them, crawling laboriously up the side of the slope. He was walking on them, tumbling and falling into the hissing mass undulating furiously beneath him.

He rolled. Down the slope, through the wet weeds and vines. Then he was struggling to get up; spiders darted and hopped, stung him in countless places. He fought them off, tore their webs away. Managed to get to his knees.

He groped for his tire iron. Where was it? Had he lost it? His fingers touched something soft. String. A ball of string. With sickened misery he pulled out handfuls of string. The tire iron had faded back. The last blow. The final symbol of his failure. He let the string fall numbly from his empty fingers.

A golem leaped on his shoulder. He saw a flash, the abrupt glint of a needle. The needle poised before his eye, an inch away, point ready to plunge deep into his brain. His arms came feebly up, then were enmeshed in foul tangles of spider web. He closed his eyes hopelessly. There was nothing left. He had failed. The battle was over. He lay waiting for the thrust . . .

# FOURTEEN

'Barton!' the golem shrilled.

He opened his eyes. The golem was busily slashing the spider webs with its needle. It speared a couple of spiders, drove the others off, then hopped back to his shoulder, close to his ear.

'Damn you,' it piped. 'I told you not to talk to anybody. This was the wrong time. Too much opposition.'

Barton blinked foolishly. His mouth opened and shut. 'Who . . . ?'

'Be still. There's only a few seconds. Your reconstruction was premature. You could have ruined everything.' The golem turned to stab a gray rat trying to reach the artery behind Barton's ear. The corpse slid slowly away, still warm and pulsing, feet twitching. 'Now get up on your feet!'

Barton struggled. 'But I don't – '

'*Hurry!* With Ahriman free there's no condition to be kept. It's no holds barred, from here on. He agreed to subject Himself to the Change, but that's over with.'

Incredulous, Barton identified the voice. It was shrill, high-pitched, but familiar. '*Mary!*' He was dumbfounded. 'But how the hell – '

The tip of her needle-sword pricked his cheek. 'Barton, you can do what has to be done. Your work is ahead.'

'Ahead?'

'He's trying to get away in his station wagon. He doesn't want his real self back. But he *must* come back! It's the only way. He's the only one with power enough.'

'No,' Barton said quietly. 'Not Meade. Not him!'

The golem's sword lifted to his eye and paused there. 'My father must be released. You have the ability.'

'Not Doctor Meade,' Barton repeated. 'I can't . . .' He shook his head numbly. '*Meade*. With his cigars and toothpick and pin-striped suit. That's where He's been!'

'It's up to you. You've seen his real shape.' Her final words cut deep into Barton. 'This is why I brought you here. Not for civic reconstruction!'

A snake slithered over Barton's foot. The golem hopped off his shoulder and started after it. Barton struggled up. The webs holding him had been cut. A whole flock of bees appeared. Day was coming. More and more bees appeared. That would take care of the golems and the rats.

In a blind daze, Barton slid and stumbled down the steep slope to the road. He peered stupidly around. Doctor Meade had managed to get his station wagon going; a mass of rats and spiders and golems and snakes covered it in a squirming curtain. Meade was feeling his way inch by inch along the road. He made the first turn, hesitated with one wheel over the lip of the edge, then righted the car and continued.

Behind him, above him, the sluggish mass that was Ahriman continued to grow. Its feelers snaked their way in a widening circle, groping, clutching, carrying things to the jelly mass. The stench was overpowering; Barton retched and retreated. It was already up to staggering proportions.

He reached the road. The car was gaining speed. It careened wildly, missed a turn, and crashed into a guide-fence. Rats and golems flew in all directions. The car shuddered, then came creakily on.

Barton hoisted a boulder. There was no other way. He'd never get through the layer of crawling gray – and the car would be past him in seconds. As it shot directly toward him he crouched, got his weight under, and hurled the big rock with all his strength.

The boulder did its job. It struck the hood of the car, bounced and skidded, and smashed through the windshield, on the left side. Glass flew everywhere. The car veered crazily – and came to a grinding, crashing halt against the base of the slope. Water and gasoline gushed from the cracked engine. Rats and spiders poured eagerly through the jagged hole in the windshield, glad of the opportunity to enter.

Meade scrambled out. Barton hardly recognized him. His face was a broken mask of terror. He ran wildly away from the station wagon, insane with fear, straight down the center of the road. His clothing was torn, skin ribboned and slashed by countless yellowed teeth. He didn't see Barton until he crashed head-on into him.

'Meade,' Barton snarled. He grabbed the staggering man by his collar and hung onto him. 'Look at me.'

Meade's vacant eyes glittered up at him, as Barton dragged him to a stop. He panted like a mute animal. No sight. No reason. He was out of his head with terror. Barton couldn't exactly blame him. An ocean of gray shapes was pouring down the road, eager for the kill. And above everything else, the vengeful shadow of Ahriman grew larger and larger.

'Barton,' Meade croaked. 'For God's sake let go of me!' He struggled to get away. 'They'll kill us. We – '

'Listen.' Barton's eyes were fixed on Meade's quivering face, only inches away. 'I know who you are. *I know who you really are.*'

The effect was instantaneous. Meade's body jerked. His mouth flew open. 'Who I – *am!*'

Barton concentrated with all his strength. He held

tight to Meade's collar and summoned each detail of the great figure, as he had first seen it, from the ledge, that morning. The majestic giant, cosmic in his silence, arms outstretched, head lost in the blazing orb of the full sun.

'Yes,' Doctor Meade said suddenly, in a strangely quiet voice.

'Meade,' Barton gasped. 'You understand? You know who you are? Do you realize – '

Meade pulled violently away. He turned awkwardly and stumbled off, down the road, hunched over like an animal. Then he stiffened. His arms flailed out, his body jerked, danced like a puppet on a wire. His face quivered. It seemed to melt and fall inward, a shapeless pool of wax.

Barton hurried after him. Meade collapsed. He rolled in agony, then leaped up. Convulsions swept over him, frenzied vibrations that snapped his limbs out, head back, reeling and falling blindly.

'Meade!' Barton shouted. He grabbed hold of the man's shoulder. The coat was smoldering; acrid fumes stung his nose, and the coat ripped away. Barton spun him around and grabbed him by the collar.

It wasn't Meade.

It wasn't anybody he'd ever seen. Or *anything* he'd ever seen. It wasn't a human being. Doctor Meade's face was gone. What had hardened and re-formed was strong and harsh. He saw it only a second. A sudden glimpse, the hawklike beak, thin lips, wild gray eyes, dilated nostrils, long sharp teeth.

A shattering roar. A cataclysmic force that mashed him flat. He was blinded. Deafened. The whole world burst loose in front of him. He was spun back, flattened. Rolled over and left behind. Smashed by a blazing fist that penetrated him and disappeared into the void beyond.

128

The void was everywhere. He was falling. He fell a long way, utterly weightless. Things drifted past him. Globes. Luminous balls. He caught at them foolishly; they ignored him and went on drifting.

Whole swarms of glowing balls flitted around him. For a time he thought they were night-flyers, gray moths that had caught fire. He slapped at them, only vaguely alarmed. More surprised than anything.

Then he noticed he was alone. And it was completely silent. But that wasn't so strange. There was nothing to make noise, no matter whatsoever. No earth. No sky. Only himself. And the steamy void.

Water was falling around him. Huge hot drops that sizzled and seared on all sides. He could feel thunder; it was too far away to hear, and anyhow, he didn't have any ears. And no eyes. He couldn't touch, either. The luminous balls continued to drift through the scorching rain; now they passed through what had been his body and calmly out the other side.

A group of the luminous balls seemed familiar. After measureless time and much thought he managed to place them.

The Pleiades.

It was suns drifting around and through him. He felt aimlessly alarmed; tried to pull himself together. But it was no use. He was spread out too far, over trillions of miles. Gaseous and vague. And slightly luminous, too. Like an extragalactic nebula. Spanning numerous star clusters, infinite systems. But how? What kept him from . . .

He was dangling. By one foot. Head downward, twisting and turning in a billowing sea of luminous particles, swarms of suns growing smaller each moment.

More and more suns swept past him on their way out of existence. Like a deflated balloon, the sphere that was the universe fizzled and danced briefly and closed in around him. Its last moments were too short to be counted; all at once it leaped wildly and vanished. The floating suns, the luminous clouds, were all gone. He was outside of the universe. Hanging by his right foot, where it had once been. Now what was there? He twisted around and tried to look up. Darkness. A form. A presence holding him.

Ormazd.

His terror was so great he couldn't speak. It was a long way down; there was no end to it. And there was no time; he'd never cease falling, if Ormazd let go. Yet, at the same instant, he knew there could be no falling, either. There was no place to fall. How could he fall?

Something gave. He clutched wildly and tried to hang on. Tried to crawl back up. Like a frightened monkey swarming up a rope. He reached, groped, begged for mercy. For pity. And he couldn't even see whom he was pleading with. Only a vast presence. A sense of being. Ormazd was there. He was *in* Ormazd. Praying piteously not to be cast out. Not to be ejected.

No time passed. But it took quite a while. His terror began to change. It transformed itself subtly. He remembered who he was. Ted Barton. Where he was. He was hanging by his right foot, beyond the universe. Who was dangling him? Ormazd, the God he had liberated.

Dull anger stirred him. He had released Ormazd. And somehow he had been swept up in Ormazd's parabola. As the God ascended, he had been yanked along.

The God was expressionless. Barton could read no feeling, no pity. But he didn't want pity. He was mad clear through. The whole thing burst loose inside him, a single thought boiling up furiously. It raged out of him loud and clear.

130

'Ormazd!' His thought clanged through the void. Reverberations echoed back, sent him vibrating. 'Ormazd!' His thought was reinforced, given body and weight; courage grew and heated his outrage. 'Ormazd, put me back!'

It had no effect.

'Ormazd!' he shouted. '*Remember Millgate!*'

Silence.

Then the presence dissolved. He fell again, down and down. Once more, luminous dots drifted through him. His being collected itself and dropped like hot rain.

And then he hit.

The impact was terrific. He bounced, shrieked with pain and was caught. Shapes formed. Heat. A blinding white flame. The sky. Trees, dark and gloomy in the early-morning twilight, yet strangely illuminated by dancing fire. The dusty road under him.

He was stretched out on his back, knocked flat. Ahriman's horde of rats and golems were swarming toward him; he could hear their claws scrabbling louder, growing into an eager din. The whole world, the Earth, its sights and sounds and smells. The scene, the moment he had left. Shady House.

No time had passed. Doctor Meade's empty husk still tottered in front of him. Still on its feet. It split and peeled back, shriveled up, discarded and forgotten. Then it slowly collapsed, a bit of charred ash, waste particles. Like everything else for yards around, it had been scorched dry, as the smoldering shaft of pure energy released itself.

'Thank God,' Barton whispered hoarsely. He staggered back and threw himself flat. The plucking feelers of filth, the extensions of Ahriman, were sliding and oozing over the side of the slope, a few yards from him. They touched the charred corpses of rats and golems and snakes

Ormazd had left behind, and then came on. They inched their way greedily toward Barton, but it was too late.

Barton crawled to a safe place, crouched, and held his breath. In the sky, the God Ormazd raced up to give battle. Ahriman snapped his extensions back like rubber bands, suddenly aware of danger. In an instant they closed, time too small to be known, distances too vast for human understanding.

The fragment, glimpsed by Barton's mortal eyes, indicated it was going to be quite a fight.

The outlines of the two gods were still dimly visible, as the sun left the mountains and began to illuminate the world.

They had grown fast. In the brief flash, like a billion suns exploding, the two gods had swept beyond the limits of the Earth. A momentary pause, and then the impact. The whole universe shuddered. They met head-on, body to body. Direct impasse, one against the other. The blazing swath that was Ormazd. The icy emptiness that was *it*, the cosmic wrecker, trying to swallow its brother and absorb Him.

It would be a long time before the battle was over. As Meade had said, probably a few more billions of years.

Bees were arriving in vast swarms. But it didn't matter much anymore. The valley – the whole Earth – had been passed by. The battleground had widened. It took in everything, every particle of matter in the universe, and perhaps beyond. Rats streaked wildly off, covered with stinging, lashing bees. Golems fled for cover and tried frantically to stab their way free. For every needle wielded by a tiny fist there were fifty angry bees. It was a losing game.

And, interestingly, some of the golems were sliding back into shapeless blobs of clay.

The snakes were the worst. Here and there the few remaining Wanderers were stoning them in the time-honored fashion. Stoning and crushing them underfoot. It did him good to see the blue-eyed, blonde-haired girl grinding a copperhead under her sharp heel. The world was getting back in its right orbit, at long last.

'Barton!' a piping voice cried, close to his foot. 'I see you were successful. Here, behind the stone. I don't want to come out until it's safe.'

'It's safe,' Barton said. He crouched down and held out his hand. 'Hop on.'

The golem came quickly out. There had been a change, even in the short time since he had last seen her. He lifted her up high, where he could get a good look at her. The morning sunlight sparkled on her bare limbs. Moist and glittering. A slim, lithe body that took his breath away.

'Hard to believe you're only thirteen,' he said slowly.

'I'm not,' was the prompt answer. She turned her supply body this way and that, to catch the light better. 'I'm ageless, Teddy dear. But I'm going to need a little outside help. There's still a strong impression by *it* on this material. Of course, that's rapidly fading.'

Barton called Christopher over. The old man limped painfully toward him. 'Barton!' he gasped. 'You're okay?'

'I'm fine. But we have a small problem here.'

She was emerging, reshaping the clay that made up her present body. But it was going to take time. The form was definitely a woman's. Not a girl's, as he remembered. But what he had known was a distortion, not the real thing.

'You're the daughter of Ormazd,' he said suddenly.

'I'm Armaiti,' the little figure answered. 'His only daughter.' She yawned, arched her slim torso, stretched

133

her slender arms. Then abruptly hopped from Barton's hand to his shoulder. 'Now, if you two will help, I'll try to regain my regular shape.'

'Like Him?' Barton was appalled. 'As large as that?'

She laughed, a tinkling, pure sound. 'No. He lives out there in the universe. I live here. Didn't you know that? He sent His only daughter here, to live on Earth. This is my home.'

'So you were the one who brought me here. Through the barrier.'

'Oh, much more than that.'

'What do you mean?'

'I sent you out of here before the Change. I'm responsible for your vacation. For every turn your car took. The flat you had when you tried to keep on the main highway to Raleigh.'

Barton grimaced. 'It took me two hours to fix that flat. Between service stations, and there was something wrong with the jack. Then it was too late to go on. We had to turn back to Richmond and spend the night.'

Armaiti's tinkling laugh sounded again. 'It was the best thing I could think of, at the time. I manipulated you here, all the way to the valley. I withdrew the barrier so you could pass in.'

'And when I tried to get out – '

'It was back, of course. It's always there, unless one or the other wishes it removed. Peter had power to come and go. So did I, but Peter never knew that.'

'You knew the Wanderers wouldn't be successful. You knew the reconstruction work, all the maps and models and charts, would fail.'

'Yes. I knew even before the Change.' Armaiti's voice was soft. 'I'm sorry, Teddy. They worked years, built and planned and slaved. But there was only one way. As long

134

as Ahriman was here, as long as the agreement was kept, and Ormazd subjected himself to its terms – '

'The town was really small stuff in all this,' Barton broke in. 'You weren't particularly concerned with it, were you?'

'Don't feel that way,' Armaiti said gently. 'It was small compared to the greater picture. But it's a *part* of the greater picture. The struggle is vast; much bigger than anything you can experience. I've never seen the real extent, myself, the final regions it's entered. Only the two of them see it as it's really waged. But Millgate is important. It was never forgotten. Only – '

'Only it had to wait its turn.' Barton was silent a moment. 'Anyhow,' he said finally, 'now I know why I was brought here.' He grinned a little. 'It's a damn good thing Peter was obliging enough to lend me his filter. Otherwise I wouldn't have had a memory to work from.'

'You did you job very well,' Armaiti said.

'And now what? Ormazd is back. They're both out there, someplace. The distortion layer is beginning to weaken. What about you?'

'I can't stay,' Armaiti said. 'If that's what you're thinking, and I know perfectly well it is.'

Barton cleared his throat, embarrassed. 'You were in human shape *once*. Can't you just sort of add a few years to – '

'Afraid not. I'm sorry. Teddy.'

'Don't call me Teddy!'

Armaiti laughed. 'All right, Mr Barton.' For a moment she touched his wrist with her tiny fingers. 'Well!' she said suddenly. 'Are you ready?'

'I guess so.' Barton reluctantly set her down. He and Christopher seated themselves on each side of her. 'What are we supposed to do? We don't know your real shape.'

There was a faint trace of sadness, almost weariness in the tinkling voice as Armaiti answered, 'I've been through many forms in my time. Every possible shape and size. Whatever you think would be the most appropriate.'

'I'm ready,' Christopher muttered.

'All right,' Barton agreed. They began their concentration, faces intense, bodies rigid. The old man's eyes bulged; his cheeks turned violet. Barton ignored him and focused his own mind with what strength he had left.

For a time nothing happened. Barton gasped for air, took another lungful, and started over. The scene in front of him, Christopher, the tiny three-inch golem, wavered and blurred.

Then slowly, imperceptibly, it began.

Maybe Christopher's imagination was superior to his own. He was a lot older; probably had more experience and time to think about it. In any case, what emerged between them utterly floored Barton. She was exquisite. Incredibly beautiful. He stopped concentrating and just gaped.

For a moment she remained between them, hands on her hips, chin high, cascades of black hair tossed back over her bare white shoulders. Flashing, sleek body, glistening in the morning sunlight. Immense dark eyes. Rippling skin. Glowing breasts, firm and upturned, as ripe as spring.

Barton closed his eyes weakly. She was the essence of generation. The bursting power of woman, of all life. He was seeing the force, the energy behind all growing things, all creativity. An unbelievably potent *aliveness* that vibrated and pulsed in radiant, shimmering waves.

That was the last he saw of her. Already, she was going. Once, he heard her laugh, rich and mellow. It lingered, but she was dissolving rapidly. Melding with the ground,

136

the trees, the sparkling bushes and vines. She flowed quickly to them, a liquid river of pure life, absorbing herself into the moist soil. He blinked, rubbed his eyes, and for a moment turned away.

When he looked again she was gone.

# FIFTEEN

It was evening. Barton slowly maneuvered his dusty yellow Packard through the streets of Millgate. He still had on his rumpled gray suit, but he had shaved, bathed and rested after the unusually strenuous night. All things considered, he felt pretty good.

As he passed the park he slowed down almost to a stop. A warm glow of satisfaction rose up inside him. A sort of personal pride. There it was. Just as it was intended to be. Part of the original plan. Back again, after all the years. And he had arranged it.

Children were romping up and down the gravel paths. One was sitting on the edge of the fountain, carefully putting his shoes back on. A couple of baby carriages. Old men, legs stuck out, rolled-up newspapers in their pockets. The sight of the people looked even better to him than the archaic Civil War cannon and the flagpole with its stars and bars.

They were the real people. The reconstruction zone, after Ahriman had left, resumed its expansion. More and more people, places, buildings, streets, were being drawn in. In a few days it would take the whole valley.

He drove back on the main drag. At one end it still said JEFFERSON STREET. But at the other end, the first wavery signpost reading CENTRAL STREET had already begun to fade into place.

There was the Bank. The old brick and concrete Millgate Merchants' Bank. Just as it had always been. The ladies' tea room was gone – forever, if things went well, out in deep space. Already, important-looking men were moving in and out through the wide doorway. And over the door, glittering in the evening sunlight, was Aaron Northrup's tire iron.

Barton continued along Central. Occasionally, the transition had produced strange results. The grocery store was only half there; the right side was Doyle's Leather Goods. A few puzzled people stood around, lost in wonder. The Change was being rolled back; it probably felt odd to walk into a store that partook of two separate worlds, one at each end.

'Barton!' a familiar voice shouted.

Barton slowed to a halt. Will Christopher burst out of the Magnolia Club, a mug of beer in one hand, a cheery grin on his weathered face. 'Hold on!' he shouted excitedly. 'My shop's coming up any second. Keep your fingers crossed!'

He was right. The hand laundry was beginning to blur. The lapping tongues were almost to it. Next door, the ancient, corroded Magnolia Club had already started to fade. Within its dying outline a different shape, a cleaner shape, arose. Christopher watched this with mixed feelings.

'I'm going to miss that joint,' he said. 'After you been hanging out in one place eighteen years – '

His beer mug vanished. And at the same time the last slatternly boards of the Magnolia Club ceased to be. Gradually, a respectable-looking shoe store wavered and began to harden into being, where the run-down bar had been.

Christopher cursed in dismay. Abruptly he found himself gripping a woman's high-heeled slipper by its strap.

'You're next,' Barton said, amused. 'There goes the hand laundry. It won't be long, now.'

He could already see the faint structure of Will's Sales and Service emerging from within. And beside him, the old man was also changing. Christopher was intent on his store; he didn't seem aware of his own alteration. His body straightened, lost its drooping sag. His skin cleared and gained a glowing flush Barton had never seen before. His eyes brightened. His hands became steadier. His dirty coat and trousers were replaced by a blue-checkered work shirt, slacks and a leather apron.

The last traces of the hand laundry faded out. It was gone – and Will's Sales and Service arrived.

Television sets sparkled in the clean, modern windows. It was a bright, up-to-date shop. A neon sign. New fixtures. Passers-by were already stopping to gaze happily at the displays; a couple of them had come along with the store. Will's Sales and Service stood out. So far, it was the most attractive shop along Central Street.

Christopher became impatient. He was eager to get inside, to his work. He restlessly fingered a screwdriver in his service belt. 'I've got a TV chassis on the bench,' he explained to Barton. 'Waiting for the picture tube to start acting up.'

'All right,' Barton said, grinning. 'You go back inside. I don't want to keep you from your work.'

Christopher eyed Barton with a friendly smile, but there was a faint shadow of doubt beginning to twitch across his good-natured features. 'Okay,' he boomed heartily. 'I'll see you, mister.'

'*Mister!*' Barton echoed, stunned.

'I know you,' Christopher murmured thoughtfully, 'but I can't quite place you.'

Sadness filled Barton. 'I'll be damned.'

'I guess I've done work for you. Know your face, but can't quite place the circumstances.'

'I used to live here.'

'You moved away, didn't you?'

'My family moved to Richmond. That was a long time ago. When I was a kid. I was born here.'

'Sure! I used to see you around. Let's see, what the hell's your name?' Christopher frowned. 'Ted something. You've grown. You were just a little fellow, in those days. Ted . . .'

'Ted Barton.'

'Sure.' Christopher stuck his hand into the car and they both shook gravely. 'Glad to see you back, Barton. You going to stay here a while?'

'No,' Barton said. 'I have to be going.'

'Through here on vacation?'

'That's right.'

'A lot of people come through here.' Christopher indicated the road; cars were already beginning to appear on it. 'Millgate's an expanding community.'

'Live-wire,' Barton said.

'Notice, my store's arranged to attract the passing motorist. I figure there's going to be more out-of-town traffic through here all the time.'

'Seems like a safe bet,' Barton admitted. He was thinking of the ruined road, the weeds, the stalled lumber truck. There'd be more traffic, all right. Millgate had been cut off eighteen years; it had plenty to make up for.

'Funny,' Christopher said slowly. 'You know, I'm sure something happened. Not very long ago. Something you and I were both involved in.'

'Oh?' Barton said hopefully.

'Had to do with a lot of people. And a doctor. Doctor Morris. Or Meade. But there's no Doctor Meade in Millgate. Just old Doc Dolan. And there were animals!'

'Don't worry about it,' Barton said, grinning a little. He started up the Packard. 'So long, Christopher.'

'Drop by, when you're through this way again.'

'I will,' Barton answered, picking up speed. Behind him Christopher waved. Barton waved back. After a moment Christopher turned and hurried eagerly back inside his radio shop. Glad to get back to work. The spreading fire had finished with him; he was fully restored.

Barton drove slowly on. The hardware store, and its crotchety, elderly owner, was gone. That pleased him. Millgate was better off without it.

His Packard passed by Mrs Trilling's boarding house. Or rather, what had once been Mrs Trilling's boarding house. Now it was an automobile sales shop. Bright new Fords behind a huge display window. Fine. Just right.

This was Millgate as it would have been, had Ahriman never showed up. The struggle still continued throughout the universe, but in this one spot, the God of Light's victory was fairly clean-cut. Not absolutely complete, perhaps. But nearly so.

He picked up speed as the Packard left town and began the long climb up the side of the mountain, toward the pass and the highway beyond. The road was still cracked and weed-covered. A sudden thought hit him; what about the barrier? Was it still there?

It wasn't. The lumber truck and its spilled cargo of logs was gone. Only a few bent weeds to show where it had been. That made him curious. What sort of laws were binding on gods? He'd never thought about it before, but obviously there were certain things gods had to do, once they had made an agreement.

As he drove around the twists and turns on the other side of the mountains, it occurred to him that Peg's twenty-four-hour deadline had run out. She was probably on her way to Richmond, by now. He knew Peg; she meant every word. The next time they met would be in a New York court of law.

Barton settled back and made himself comfortable against the warm seat. It wouldn't be possible to go back to his life, the way it was. Peg was out. All *that* was finished and done. He might as well face it.

And anyhow, Peg seemed a little dull, everything considered.

He was recalling a sleek, glowing body. A lithe shape diffusing itself into the moist soil of early morning. A flash of black hair and eyes as she trickled away from him, into the Earth which was her home. Red lips, white teeth. A gleaming flicker of bare limbs – and then she was gone.

Gone? Armaiti wasn't gone. She was everywhere. In all the trees, in the green fields and lakes and forest lands. The fertile valleys and mountains on all sides of him. She was below and around him. She filled up the whole world. She lived there. Belonged there.

Two swelling mountains divided for the road ahead. Barton passed slowly between them. Firm hills, rich and full, identical peaks glowing warmly in the late-afternoon sun.

Barton sighed. He'd be seeing reminders of her just about everywhere.

## DR. BLOODMONEY

Dr. Bloodmoney is a post-nuclear-holocaust masterpiece filled with a host of Dick's most memorable characters: Hoppy Harrington, a deformed mutant with telekinetic powers; Walt Dangerfield, a self-less disc jockey stranded in a satellite circling the globe; Dr. Bluthgeld, the megalomaniac physicist largely responsible for the decimated state of the world; and Stuart McConchie and Bonnie Keller, two unremarkable people bent on the survival of goodness in a world devastated by evil. Epic and alluring, this brilliant novel is a mesmerizing depiction of Dick's undying hope in humanity.

Fiction/Science Fiction/0-375-71929-6

## FLOW MY TEARS, THE POLICEMAN SAID

Television star Jason Taverner is so famous that 30 million viewers eagerly watch his prime-time show until one day, all proof of his existence is erased. And in the claustrophobic betrayal state of *Flow My Tears, the Policeman Said*, loss of proof is synonymous with loss of life. As Taverner races to solve the riddle of his "disappearance" the author immerses us in a horribly plausible United States in which everyone informs on everyone else, a world in which even the omniscient police have something to hide. His bleakly beautiful novel bores into the deepest bedrock of the self and plants a stick of dynamite at its center.

Fiction/Science Fiction/0-679-74066-X

## THE THREE STIGMATA OF PALMER ELDRITCH

Not too long from now, when exiles from a blistering Earth huddle miserably in Martian colonies, the only things that make life bearable are the drugs. A new substance called Chew-Z is marketed under the slogan: "God promises eternal life. We can deliver it." The question is: What kind of eternity? And who—or what—is the deliverer? In this wildly disorienting funhouse of a novel, Dick explores mysteries that were once the property of St. Paul and Aquinas. His wit, compassion, and knife-edged irony make this novel as moving as it is visionary.

Fiction/Science Fiction/0-679-73666-2

## THE MAN IN THE HIGH CASTLE

It's America in 1962. Slavery is legal once again. The few Jews who still survive hide under assumed names. In San Francisco, the *I Ching* is as common as the Yellow Pages. All because some 20 years earlier the United States lost a war—and is now occupied jointly by Nazi Germany and Japan. This harrowing, Hugo Award–winning novel is the work that established Philip K. Dick as an innovator in science fiction while breaking the barrier between science fiction and the serious novel of ideas. In it, Dick offers a haunting vision of history as a nightmare from which it may just be possible to awake.

Fiction/Science Fiction/0-679-74067-8

## THE SIMULACRA

Set in the middle of the twenty-first century, *The Simulacra* is the story of an America where the whole government is a fraud and the President is an android. Against this backdrop Dr. Superb, the sole remaining psychotherapist, is struggling to practice in a world full of the maladjusted. Ian Duncan is desperately in love with the first lady, who he has never met. Richard Kongrosian refuses to see anyone because he is convinced that his body odor is lethal. And the fascistic Bertold Goltz is trying to overthrow the government. With wonderful aplomb, Dick brings this story to a crashing conclusion and in classic fashion shows there is always another layer of conspiracy beneath the one we see.

Fiction/Science Fiction/0-375-71926-1

## UBIK

Glen Runciter is dead. Or is everybody else? *Someone* died in an explosion orchestrated by Runciter's business competitors. And, indeed, Runciter's funeral is scheduled in Des Moines. But in the meantime, his mourning employees are receiving bewildering—and sometimes scatological—messages from their boss. And the world around them is warping in ways that suggest that their own time is running out. Or already has. This searing metaphysical comedy of death and salvation is a tour de force of paranoiac menace and unfettered slapstick, in which the departed give business advice, shop for their next incarnation, and run the continual risk of dying yet again.

Fiction/Science Fiction/0-679-73664-6

## GALACTIC POT-HEALER

The Glimmung wants Joe Fernwright. Fernwright is a pot-healer—a repairer of ceramics—in a drably utilitarian future where such skills have little value. And the Glimmung? The Glimmung is a being that looks something like a gyroscope, something like a teenaged girl, and something like the contents of an ocean. What's more, it may be divine. And, like certain gods of old Earth, it has a bad temper. What could a seemingly omnipotent entity want with a humble pot-healer? Combining quixotic adventure, spine-chilling horror, and deliriously paranoid theology, *Galactic Pot-Healer* is a voyage to alternate worlds of the imagination.

Fiction/Science Fiction/0-679-75297-8


## MARTIAN TIME-SLIP

On the arid colony of Mars the only thing more precious than water may be a ten-year-old schizophrenic boy named Manfred Steiner. For although the UN has slated "anomalous" children for deportation and destruction, other people—especially Supreme Goodmember Arnie Kott of the Water Worker's union—suspect that Manfred's disorder may be a window into the future. But what sort of future? And what happens to those unfortunates whom Manfred ushers into it? In *Martian Time-Slip* Dick uses power politics, extraterrestrial real estate scams, adultery, and murder to penetrate the mysteries of being and time.

Fiction/Science Fiction/0-679-76167-5


## A SCANNER DARKLY

Cops and criminals have always been interdependent, but no novel has explored this symbiosis more powerfully than *A Scanner Darkly*. Bob Arctor is a dealer of the lethally addictive drug Substance D. Fred is the police agent assigned to bust him. To do so, Fred takes on the identity of a drug dealer named Bob Arctor. And since Substance D—which Arctor takes in massive doses—gradually splits the user's brain into two distinct, combative entities, Fred doesn't realize he is narcing on himself. Caustically funny, eerily accurate in its depiction of junkies and the walking brain-dead, Philip K. Dick's industrial-grade stress test of identity is as unnerving as it is enthralling.

Fiction/Science Fiction/0-679-73665-4

# VALIS

*VALIS* is the first book in Dick's incomparable final trio of novels, which also includes *The Divine Invasion* and *The Transmigration of Timothy Archer*. This disorienting and bleakly funny work is about a schizophrenic hero named Horselover Fat; the hidden mysteries of Gnostic Christianity; and reality as revealed through a pink laser. Hailed as "a joy to read" by *The Washington Post Book World*, *VALIS* is a theological detective story, in which God is both a missing person and the perpetrator of the ultimate crime.

Fiction/Science Fiction/0-679-73446-5

## ALSO AVAILABLE

VINTAGE BOOKS
Available at your local bookstore, or call toll-free to order:
1-800-793-2665 (credit cards only).